Reviews for **The Watcher**.

A delightfully witty story blending farce, black humour, a strong thoughtful plot and rich characterisation into a gourmet novel. Star Dancer has a draining presence and, to the inhabitants of the planet Ojal, this is a life threatening situation. Earth is identified as the planet from which Star Dancer comes. The Ojaliens, with expert help, produce an android, Kybion, and send it into the past to wait for the rise of Star Dancer and prevent it from draining Ojal's power. Excellent.

SFF Books

Refreshingly devoid of any serious social, moral, human or extra-terrestrial issue, Jane Palmer's The Watcher (Women's Press, £2.50) flips lightly around the adventures of an Asian teenage girl with no nerves, helped along by a Benson-from-Soap character and an ugly baddie who gets fried by the power source he is trying to steal. If the baddies succeed then an entire planet of one-parent families with wings will perish; but, fear not, most of the action takes place in English villages by the sea. It has the tone of early Eric Frank Russell and a style reminiscent of Enid Blyton.

Josephine Saxton New Statesman

...Jane Palmer's *The Watcher* turns some of these clichés around and her cast list features a middle-aged black android who falls in love with a middle-aged female humanoid. The watcher of the title is a benevolent 17-year-old young woman, which knocks your aging male warlords into the box marked 'disposable', methinks.

Adele Saleem 7 Days

First published in Great Britain
by The Women's Press 1986
As **The Watcher**

This edition by Dodo Books 2008

Copyright © Jane Palmer 2008

ISBN 978-1-906442-17-0

Other science fiction books by this author

THE PLANET DWELLER
NIGHTINGALE
THE ATON BIRD
MOVING MOOSEVAN
BABEL'S BASEMENT

THE
KYBION

First published in 1986
by The Women's Press as
THE WATCHER

Jane Palmer

DODO BOOKS

CHAPTER 1

The stars sparkled through the dense atmosphere as the yellow sun set. It would be a few moments before the other sun appeared above the horizon. Controller Opu shut down the refractor that had been concentrating the nutritional radiation into the energy pool below. The rising sun's pink light had no nourishment value. Its luminosity was just as great, bathing everything in a pretty pallor, yet it was the yellow binary star that had given the ancient races the energy they needed to evolve and create their civilisation.

The first refractor able to collect and store the sun's energy had been built three million years ago; or so it was believed, because any trace of it had vanished long ago. Since then the efficiency of these technological temples had increased a thousandfold. Unfortunately, Ojalie ambition had not. To them, the greatest delight of these gigantic silver domes was the way in which they spangled the planet like a pomander studded with pearls.

Opu tucked her wings comfortably by her sides. Looking over her blunt beak that ran seamlessly down from her cranium, she pondered on the glinting shields that were slowly closing as the pink sun rose above the horizon. She wondered where the Ojalie would be now without the light energy from those massive pools to bathe in when they needed the occasional boost. Perhaps soaring above the cloudbanks to collect their nourishment on the wing when the yellow sun disappeared behind them, or maybe chewing different plants to see if they could digest them. That would have been pretty pointless. The Ojalie had never developed the bowels to cope with solid food. Intestines and other internal organs would just increase the weight this species had to get airborne. The only other

nutrition their digestive tracts required was a mineral-
rich fluid that bubbled from the crust of their planet,
though over the millennia some other potions had been
invented. These were responsible for more mid-air
collisions than freak air currents.

Most of the space inside the short, wide-hipped
bodies of the Ojalie was to allow their large-skulled
offspring to grow. Their pelvic girdles were so wide
they were unable to walk very well, but their huge
wings more than compensated for this until the last
stages of pregnancy when they were grounded. It had
never occurred to anyone that there was pleasure in
walking very far anyway. As the Ojalie were
hermaphrodite, this shape was pretty standard, even
between different racial types that hadn't interbred.
Without that exchange of genes, and the ability to both
inseminate and give birth, they would have probably
evolved back into the pigeon like creature found in
ancient fossils.

Opu looked down at the chattering bundle of unco-
ordinated wings, arms, and legs tumbling about the
floor beneath everyone's feet, and wondered what pitch
of evolution she represented. Her child had just
managed to escape from the play-pen that was
supposed to be child-proof for the fifth time, and was
about to bite the leg of another controller to discover
the different things a beak could be used for. If Opu
had known how lively Opuna was going to be, and how
many friends she was going to alienate, she would
have thought twice about having her.

Her gene partner, Anapa, had not so long ago
looked thoughtfully at the antics of the bundle of
disruption and observed, 'How does she manage to be
so active? Mine hardly moves about at all.'

'Swap?' Opu had suggested hopefully.

'Not now I've got my home just how I like it,' was
the prompt reply. 'I might let you visit us when she

runs out of energy and has more control over her hands and beak'

'A fine parent you are.'

'Maybe, but I'm sure she has more of your genes than mine.'

Anapa's disposition was about as vivacious as the grey-skinned, fungus eating slow-worm, so Opu had to agree.

The unfortunate controller let out a shriek as the monster child's beak found her leg and she turned, only to find an innocent Opu looking in amazement at her child's behaviour.

Finishing the shift under the frosty disapproval of her colleagues, Opu tucked her squawking offspring beneath her short arm and leisurely flew back to the devastation of her own home. As things would immediately be dislodged and flung about as soon as they had been tidied up, she had long since stopped bothering and only invited in the most broad-minded of her friends. She had thought about cutting down the amount of light nourishment Opuna received. Many, who claimed to be more responsible, had frowned severely at the idea. All growing children needed at least five meals every sun. Without it they would shrivel up to nothing as their ancestors, so deprived, had done. Or just fall to pieces, like the pioneering astronauts when they had travelled too far from the sun. The Ojalie were one of those species dependent, like most vegetation, on their sun. They had given up trying to leave their planet, but the old stories of what had happened to the early astronauts still made Opu shudder.

Perhaps her offspring wouldn't be a pest forever. A long walk to try and tire Opuna into flying only exhausted her and left the brat as ebullient as ever. They watched a golden backed reptile disembowel an unsuspecting mollusc, and then spit out its shell. Opu felt ill, while Opuna pondered the need to fly when such wonders could be seen on the ground.

Opu asked herself what she had been like at that age, and had to believe the horror stories her parent had told about her juvenile behaviour.

They next came upon an automatic cleanser scraping up the remains of some poor pulverised creature that had fallen from the sky. Opu decided Opuna's flying lesson had lasted long enough. She scooped the brat up and flew back home where she placed the child in the cubicle to be bathed in the life-giving sun's light, while she sprawled out and fanned herself with a wing. The one positive thing about having a monster for an offspring was that it took her mind off other problems.

As Opu fanned her cares away she recalled the wispy shape that had hovered over the refractor two shifts ago. She had put it down to the exhaustion brought on by parenthood. That was it! She could make a reasonable request for a temporary parental swap. Anapa had been avoiding it for ages, now she could face a fine if she refused.

So Anapa was compelled to ensure the rigors of Opuna's delinquency while Opu took the other child of the union, Anop. At last there was an offspring she could place in the control room playpen without having to worry about what disaster she was about to engineer. Opu felt relaxed. Her colleagues began to speak to her again, and she was no longer tired.

Then the energy level indicator dived for a second. She glanced out at the open shields and saw a menacing shape hovering over the refractor. This time it was blazing intensely, like a small sun. Inside the flaming shell a shape slowly revolved, growing brighter and brighter with the power it consumed from the energy pool.

One of the controllers jumped in alarm. 'Vian

Solran! Star Dancer!'

Opu instinctively hit the lever that opened the power bank to the other stations dotted about the planet before the level could fall dangerously low.

The usually laid-back Ojalie were thrown into a panic that made worldwide gossip. The controllers would have liked to blame Opu for the power drain, but on this occasion her conduct was too efficient to fault. However despicable her brat, she was the only one with the know-how and presence of mind when it was needed.

'Vian Solran, Star Dancer,' Opu mused to herself when the emergency was over. It was strange how such ancient race memories could surface when someone was under stress. Given the circumstances, it was probably the most logical thing anyone could say about the energy vampire. For all their knowledge and expertise, it might as well have been that star-devouring deity.

Legend had it that Vian Solran was a born from a quasar at the centre of the Galaxy when it was young, and developed the rapacious appetite of a collapsar. It was believed the entity could appear anywhere in space and perform a deadly dance from one star to the next, devouring each in turn.

That was the first visit of the energy vampire to Ojal. As yet, it hadn't become as dangerous as Vian Solran, but the unspoken fear that it was only a matter of time grew. Long before the Star Dancer turned its attention to their suns, the planet's energy pools would be bled dry and the Ojalie doomed. Despite their technical competence, no one had yet dared put that fear into words. Like a blip on the solar scan, or disease in the digestive tracts of the perverse creatures that decided to survive off vegetation, it first had to be investigated.

The controllers had been so stunned by the

sighting they weren't able to describe it when making out a report. Even the children watching from their playpen couldn't invent words to express what they had seen, though Opu didn't doubt for one moment that Opuna would have found several.

When she returned for the next shift, inventive suggestions from every source had been pouring in to explain the apparition seen by the staff of Main Base Station 93 - usually such a lucid bunch. No convincing explanation could be found amongst them. On Ojal, monsters were things of the remote past. They knew of no hostile civilisations wanting to attack their planet, yet the Star Dancer must have been alien.

The only good thing to come of the traumatic event for Opu was that Anapa now had to look after both children while she waited with the other controllers for the Star Dancer to appear again. Even a small drain on an energy pool caused a planet wide imbalance, and there was a limit to how much the other stations could compensate for it.

As though it knew they were waiting, the Star Dancer's next appearance was at a refractor on the other side of Ojal. Although the staff had been prepared for a drain on the energy pool, they were watching for something terrifying, not beautiful. To their amazement a huge ghostly butterfly floated over their open shields, sucking power from the energy pool like nectar from a blossom. This time the power drain was serious.

From then on the lives of Opu and her gene partner became even more complicated. Anapa's, because she was obliged to look after both children, monstrous and docile, indefinitely, and Opu's because the computer, which took no account of anyone's delinquency, decided that she was the best controller to take charge of the situation. A sudden promotion her easy-going nature could have done without.

Space travel might have been biologically impossible for the Ojalie; transmitting signals at tachyon frequencies was not. Unable to visually observe the sky because their suns permanently lit the planet, they had designed spacecraft that could carry satellites far beyond Ojal to orbit with the comets. They achieved this not long after constructing the first refractors about three million years ago. Since then they had developed the technology to see and track anything within the known Galaxy. Something many species accomplished at space travel weren't able to do. This Ojalie expertise, and a willingness to share it, had made them popular with other civilisations, which was just as well. They were going to need help as the Star Dancer's visits increased and their life giving power was drained away.

CHAPTER 2

Opu, as new controller-in-charge, was still unable to make sense of the multi-form Star Dancer after its sixteenth visit. She decided, because it was energy, they would be able to pinpoint its origin. By the time a way was devised of attaching a tracking signal to the tail of the marauding manifestation, the situation had become critical. When the opportunity to use it arose, the signal only managed to follow the apparition as far as the edge of the binary star system, and then the entity accelerated beyond the speed of light and shook it off. No one had been expecting this. Though the Ojalie could talk to the other side of the Galaxy in real time, not many manifestations with mass were known to travel at the speed of thought.

Opu was beginning to feel like a wrung-out beak warmer. She sent a message around the planet to rally the technicians to generate enough power to create a tachyon "tag" that could pursue the Star Dancer at the speed of thought. If it travelled any faster than that she resolved to give it in her notice and fade away with everyone else.

As Opu waited, it didn't help to receive a hysterical message from Anapa. Opuna had succeeded in alienating most of her friends, and sent the remainder into a near frenzy as they tried to relieve her of the menace for a few hours. The controller-in-charge had other things on her mind, though.

Opu felt a relieving numbness creep over her as they waited for the thirsty apparition's next visit. At least it made the waiting easier. She checked that every available satellite was programmed to track the tachyon tag, across the Universe if need be. It would have been pointless to ask assistance of any world until they knew where it led them. All they could do was wait.

Without warning, the Star Dancer was there, hovering above Station 30 at the planet's equator. This time it was shaped like a long-legged insect draped in swirling robes. While the controllers topped up the energy pool from other stations, Opu transmitted the tag. It tracked the intruder as it rapidly retreated into space. To her relief, it worked this time.

By the time the Star Dancer had reached the other side of the Galaxy, snippets of information began to filter in. There was no sensible time sequence to their arrival and the jumble was fed into the computer to unscramble: it produced data measuring a planet's location, density, size, and atmosphere. More data produced images, some easy to comprehend, and others that had to be electronically translated before they made sense. At least they could be sure that the Star Dancer came from another world and wasn't an emanation from some freak star - the name stuck anyway. Now it was possible to contact the planets in that region and glean more specific information about the solar system.

As they could make instantaneous contact across light years with anyone who had receivers capable of picking up their signal, the Ojalie had given up using electromagnetic radiation waves for communication millennia ago. Opu soon learnt that their quarry inhabited the third planet of a yellow sun that appeared to have a small, dim red companion. The world's landmass was verdant, and filled with a multitude of life forms.

An aquatic species on Taigal Rax, in a neighbouring solar system, had long been interested in the Star Dancer's world. Taigalians were more concerned about the large body of water that covered most of the planet, which they had named Perimeter 84926, than the creatures that had managed to crawl out of it. As they believed the oceans of the Star Dancer's home would eventually cover the remaining landmasses, just as they had done on Taigal Rax, their priority was to learn more about the evolving species in the water than the eventually-to-be-drowned ones out of it. They did send Opu some useful data, however.

A precocious land animal had rapidly evolved to become reasonably intelligent. Unlike the Ojalie, who had six limbs, this animal and other larger life forms had only four and there, mostly, appeared to be two sexes. On the verge of space exploration, this planet had launched a vehicle carrying odd information about their world and a small plaque representing one of the larger sex making a sign of some sort with an upper limb. The creature was known to have a fear/aggression response, and to be terrified of anything out of its immediate experience.

Opu groaned. 'Very helpful. Contacting them is definitely out.'

'No chance they could be sending the creature

deliberately, if they are aggressive?' somebody suggested.

'With their backward technology?' Opu didn't even bother to turn and see who had spoken.

She sat back and thought. Their only chance lay with the aquatic species on Taigal Rax. They may have been more interested in this planet's oceans, but knew about the terrestrial creatures inhabiting Perimeter 84926, and were closer to it than any comparably advanced civilisation. They even had laboratories deep in the planet's crust and could activate slumbering service robots at the bottom of its oceans.

Hardly aware that she had come to a decision, Opu transmitted a detailed summary of their predicament to Taigal Rax. She next sent out for engineers to design an android to track the Star Dancer on its own planet.

As soon as the others knew what she was about to do, the chorus of controllers, who secretly believed they could do the job better, arose. 'There isn't time for that.'

'There will be.' Opu didn't have the patience to elaborate. 'Somebody find me Technician Controller Annac.'

'She's dead - or retired.'

Unable to breathe in the hothouse of objections generated by little more than controlled hysteria, Opu stepped out onto the balcony, unfurled her wings, and took off into the cool pink sky without a word of explanation or apology.

Below, amongst the spacious gardens, rambling, twisting homes punctuated the skyline in a haphazard fashion. The older Ojalies lived here, out of the flight paths of the younger more reckless fliers, and whiled away their time doing anything that age, advanced technology and their fancy allowed.

Opu's purple-scaled tunic was impossible to miss as she hovered over the flat roof of one home, catching the attention of the figure seated on it.

Controller Annac glanced up as though not really amazed at the visit from the senior controller who held the fate of the planet in her hands. 'Thought it about time you retired too, young Opu?'

Opu touched down beside Annac. 'I'm tired of promotion, children, and monstrous apparitions that drop in from the other side of the Galaxy.'

'So you should retire. Though I thought you went in for a youngster? What's she like?'

'A brat.'

'Oh. Some are you know.'

'Problem with retiring, though, is that...' Opu took a deep breath, and stopped.

'Is that?'

'Is that nobody else will be living to retirement age if you can't help me with a small problem,' Opu managed to say without sounding too overcome at the thought of it herself.

Annac put aside the plan of the force field bubble she had been working on. It looked as though sending goods by sunbeams would have to wait. 'I wouldn't call that a small problem. What do you want me to do?'

'A long while ago you devised a system for transmitting matter from one place to another. It could be sent faster than light without the need for a receiver.'

Annac gave her a long, hard look with her large orange eyes. 'You mean the one that used the Kybini particle?'

'That's it. The elementary particle without any mass.'

'I withdrew the proposal for the Kybini System.'

'I know,' said Opu.

'Then you know why.'

'I do. But it's not my intention to transmit people with it.'

'Even if I'm sure you won't, how can I be sure no one else will? Mineral matter was what it was intended for, not us.'

'We've run out of options. Delicate sensibilities are for the unthreatened and comfortable. The Ojalie have never confronted extinction. The Star Dancer isn't a comet we can deflect.'

Opu's tone had enough gravity to make Annac bend her moral stance.

'Is it really that bad?'

'A few more energy drains and the whole system will bleed to death. We're all three million years too evolved to go back to basking in the sun. Come and see for yourself if you don't believe me.'

Annac sighed. So much for a peaceful retirement. 'All right. But if you want to reach the source of this thing on the other side of the Galaxy with my system, you're not going to have much success. It's only effective under distances of two hundred light years. Over that, it's impossible to select the time matter arrives. It could take ages.'

'Our computer signal doesn't though,' Opu hinted. She could see Annac would remain unconvinced until she explained her plan.

The controllers weren't surprised to see Opu and Annac stroll in from the balcony and go to the plans the android engineers had produced.

'We've got enough data to make a transmitter. We'll use its energy imprint to create a signal that will attract the Star Dancer on its own planet. The data can be sent with the components for an android.'

Annac pointed to the blueprint. 'What's this machine going to look like then?' There was something aesthetically unpleasant about it. 'There's no outer casing,' she complained,

'Doesn't matter. Will its components transmit on your system?'

'Of course, but not at this range.'

'Good.' Opu smiled beneath her blunt beak. 'Let's hope that any favours Ojal has done in the past were appreciated. The Taigalians have already promised to help.'

'How far away from this Perimeter 84926 are they?'

'One hundred and fifty light years.'

'Then if they transmit the android, it'll arrive far too soon, even with compensations for different space time.'

'Over one of Perimeter 84926's centuries before it actually happens here,' Opu explained, 'This will give the android time to orientate itself and be established when the energy source manifests itself there - I hope.'

'You'll have no control over the machine,' Annac warned. 'We can only transmit it back into their past because the signal will bisect the time curve Perimeter 84926 has travelled through.'

'Of course we won't have any control over it. The first thing we'll know about it intercepting the Star Dancer is when it stops appearing here.'

'And how will that pile of metal and crystal manage to do that?'

'We intend our aquatic friends to build into this expensive pile of metal and crystal a sense of what the creatures on Perimeter 84926 look like, and then use your Kybini system to transmit it. They can supply it with power units and any data needed about the planet. The android will be able to change its appearance whenever it needs... and develop living tissue if necessary.'

The other controllers froze in horror.

'Living tissue!' Annac blurted out. 'If you're sending something like that back into anyone's history

without any control over it, you'd better pray the
Watchers never find out.'

'We'll double-check it, and Taigal Rax shall do the
same. It'll only activate the biological process if they
instruct it. We have to take the risk. We've got
everything to lose if we don't.'

However tedious she found retirement, Annac
knew she had no right to obstruct other Ojalies from
having a future. 'So we'll only know whether it has
been successful when the entity stops attacking the
energy pools?'

'Assuming I start transmitting the data before
things get out of hand here, just so.' Opu started to
transmit the program to Taigal Rax.

Annac cursed as her old wings fluttered her
unsurely home into the pink sunrise. 'What a way to
spend retirement.'

CHAPTER 3

A heavy mist rolled across the inky sea washing
against the treacherous rocks. The moon lit the grey
chalk cliffs where the breeze had pushed the mist back,
and they glowed like a sinister silver ribbon.

Above the fuming waves an eerie, swishing noise
echoed about the top of the cliffs. It was followed by an
unlikely tinkling sound as something hit the ground. A
couple of seconds passed. Another swishing was
followed by the tinkling sound. Then again and again
until there was an untidy heap of diamond-metal,
crystal, and gold tendons on a cushion of sea thrift and
twitch-grass.

Delivery complete, the glinting components began
to arrange themselves. Some stood erect as though
trying to take their bearings and others rolled towards
their adjoining members. Each piece knew where it
should fit, like a mechanical chromosome. Clicking and

whirring, they assembled themselves into a glittering, faceless machine. It sat twinkling on top of the cliff for several moments, checking its components and circuits, then lifted itself erect on two stick-like legs in imitation of a human frame.

It picked its way unsurely over the unfamiliar ground towards the edge of the cliff and sent out signals in every direction to make take its bearings, then stood pondering for a few seconds.

Satisfied, it sprang forward and plunged into the dark churning sea below.

***

An ominous rumble echoed from the bowels of the ironclad ship as its cargo slid across the hold. The vessel tilted so far over the deck was partly submerged. The sails and the steam-driven paddles of the merchantman were useless in the teeth of the storm that was trying to capsize it. The crew were well rehearsed for such a disaster. They had been expecting something like it for their last eight voyages. They didn't begrudge the owners their insurance money, but they were damned if they were going to drown for it. Before the order to abandon ship could be given, the lifeboats were launched and passengers and crew loaded into them. When someone yelled across the bows to ask the inebriated captain if he was going down with his ship, he sobered up with remarkable alacrity and slid across the deck to join his first mate in the nearest boat.

'Sheer off! Sheer off!' he yelled. 'Sheer off or we'll all be sucked down with her!' as though that hadn't already occurred to the sailors battling with oars.

'My cargo! My cargo!' rang out a despairing cry from one of the smaller boats being rowed away from the mêlée towards the cliffs looming out of the spray.

'Better to be alive and have the insurance,' a young

man hauling at an oar tried to reassure Mr Humbert.

'I don't need your insolence, you young pup!'

'Well shut up then you old fool, and sit down,' snapped an older woman. 'If you can't help row the boat you might stop rocking it.'

Mr Humbert was obviously not used to being spoken to in such a manner and would have stood resolutely at the bows glowering if a wave hadn't thrown him down to the bottom of the boat.

The young woman pulling at the other oar snatched a glance over her shoulder. 'We're heading straight for the cliffs, Toby! We should have taken a sailor on board with us.'

'You're right, Tasmin!' The young man was exhausted and panicking. 'We're being dragged towards them! I'm more used to holding a pen than an oar.'

At that the older woman placed herself between the struggling younger couple and, seizing the end of each oar, tried to add her weight to their efforts. Humbert meanwhile sat facing them, staring stonily at their exertion as though his Victorian affluence had given him some immunity against drowning.

Soon all the other lifeboats with sailors on board were out of sight and in safer waters. As much as the three battled with the waves, the cliffs were soon towering above them and the boat was sucked towards their craggy walls.

One of the oars snapped against the jagged rocks. 'Get down!' yelled the older woman. 'Lie flat!'

All four clung to the slats in the bottom of the flooded boat as it banged against one rock after another. At any moment they expected it to disintegrate and pitch them into the swirling water.

Then the hammering suddenly stopped. The roaring torrent was left behind and they were swept into a world of muffled darkness. Ahead was the gushing of water being forced into a large chamber. For a few seconds they were spun round, and then the boat travelled along a straight channel.

'We're in a tunnel,' the older woman eventually murmured.

'I'm scared, Mrs Angel,' whispered Toby. 'Are you all right, Tasmin?'

'I'd rather be in here than outside.' Tasmin rose from the bottom of the boat to see if she could glimpse anything through the pitch-blackness and banged her head on the cave roof.

'Be careful,' Mrs Angel warned. 'We could be travelling into a dead end.'

'What can we do?' asked Toby helplessly.

'It depends on how narrow the tunnel is. We may be able to wall-walk our way out once this storm has abated.'

'You mean like the canal bargees?'

'Yes, like the canal bargees.'

'Goodness. My legs would never be long enough.'

'You're an inadequate sort of creature aren't you? What made you think you would be a suitable husband for my assistant?'

'Please, Mrs Angel, it's hardly the time and place to discuss that,' remonstrated Tasmin.

'This is the sort of situation that will prove how worthy he really is.'

'But you can't expect Toby to be the one to rescue us.'

'Then you might have at least considered a more suitable specimen to break your vestal vow for, young lady - a ledger clerk indeed!'

'How can I keep that vow forever?'

'You will for as long as I employ you. Our class of clientele will not want to listen to their departed loved ones through the mouth of a housewife or scarlet woman.'

'I'm sure I wouldn't do anything to dishonour Tasmin, Mrs Angel,' protested Toby.

'Fortunately, so am I.'

The argument would have continued if an eerily glimmering light hadn't appeared ahead of them. They were swept out of the tunnel into a large dimly lit cave. At the far end was a wide platform. The boat came alongside it and was nudged to a stop.

Gratefully, the sodden passengers clambered out. Before them was a wall studded with small lights and knobs. Some of the rock was transparent and inside it were cavities holding strange machines, spinning, and clicking in time to some tuneless rhythm.

Astonished at what they had accidentally transgressed into, no one spoke. They gingerly examined their surroundings, careful not to touch anything. The thought crossed their minds that they could be trapped here for a long time.

A sickly light appeared in the water lapping the platform. A shape was walking towards them from its depths. Although the creature carried itself like a human being, its movements were mechanical. As it rose from the water the travellers shrank to the far end of the platform. The entity wore a long shroud, like a monk's habit, which instantly dried when the air touched it as it walked up some rough steps and onto the platform, cutting off their only chance of escaping in the boat.

Even the indomitable Mrs Angel was daunted by the strange hooded figure. 'Who are you?' she demanded tremulously.

'Who are *you?*' the figure asked in a metallic, clicking voice.

'I am Mrs Angel.' Despite her apprehension, she formally introduced the others in turn as though she were at a dinner party, 'This is Tasmin, and Mr Humbert. And we call this fair-haired young man

Toby. He's only a ledger clerk.' She turned back to the figure. 'Now, what is your name?'

'I am the Kybion,' it replied.

'Rum sort of name,' muttered Toby.

Only one thing concerned the entity. 'What are you doing here?'

'Why ask that?' snapped Mrs Angel. 'You must already know.' She wasn't sure what made her say it.

'You are right, Mrs Angel,' the voice clicked in what might have been surprise. 'You are perceptive.'

'I am a medium.'

The Kybion didn't seem to register the meaning of the word, so she explained, 'I can see into the future and contact spirits from the world of the dead.'

As that revelation met with stony silence, Tasmin added, 'Mrs Angel and I were coming back from France after an important séance when our ship foundered.'

'Wretched ironclads,' snorted Mr Humbert. 'How can anything stay afloat with all that metal riveted to it?'

'Remember the insurance, Mr Humbert,' Toby dared to remind him, and received a hefty clip round the ear for his advice.

Before real violence could break out, the Kybion's voice resonated about the cave. 'You should all be dead.'

'Probably so,' agreed Mrs Angel. 'But the Good Lord in his infinite mercy spared us.'

'Your "Good Lord" had nothing to do with the matter, Mrs Angel. I made the inlet you were swept into. It was pure chance your boat found it. You should have all been killed on the cliff-face. Events cannot be moved out of time sequence.'

'What do you mean, sir?' Humbert strode towards the mysterious gowned figure. 'Do you know who I am?'

'You should be dead, Mr Humbert,' was the clinical

reply.

At that, Humbert's heavily-jowled face glowed red with fury. 'Now let's see who you are, sir! This mumbo jumbo has gone far enough!' He reached out and snatched off the Kybion's hood. Its habit fell open.

Mr Humbert reeled back in terror and toppled from the platform.

The other three looked on in horrified disbelief, ignoring Humbert's calls for help as he splashed about in the shallow water. Standing before them was a faceless jumble of tangled wire tendons, and winking crystal arteries. The creature was a metal skeleton entwined with gold nerves, and supported by clear muscles filled with fluorescing fluid. Not even Mrs Angel could think of anything to say to that.

'I am the Kybion,' the machine announced. 'I am not yet whole.'

'You're really going to kill us, aren't you?' said Tasmin as the trembling Toby wrapped his short arms protectively about her.

'The fault that you did not die is mine.'

'We don't mind - really we don't,' blurted out Toby.

'I am from a future time. I cannot interfere with the history of this planet, even to let you live.'

'You are a scoundrel, sir!' spluttered Humbert, dragging himself back onto the platform. 'Not only a scoundrel, but as twisted a piece of machinery as is ever liable to be assembled by a madman.'

'And no one can travel from the future,' snapped Mrs Angel. 'It would be ungodlike if they could.'

'I am the Kybion. I have no gods. This God of yours is part of your own inadequacy in working out existence for yourself. Many stars away, people can achieve what you call miracles. They do not need gods. I come from them.'

Tasmin disengaged herself from Toby to square up to the machine. 'Why?'

'I was sent to stop a creature they call Star Dancer
from sucking the life energy from another planet. At
some time in the future it will originate from this
world. I am here to wait for it.'

'Why not let us help you instead of killing us?'
pleaded Toby. 'What possible harm could we do to the
future if you were to let us live?'

The Kybion hesitated. 'If I were to let you help me,
I would have to prolong your lives for longer than is
natural to your species. How can I be sure you would
not try to disrupt the future of this world if I did that?'

'We could only give you our word,' Tasmin
reluctantly admitted.

'On this cross,' Mrs Angel pulled a large crucifix
from her sodden blouse.

'Yes, yes,' begged Humbert. 'We couldn't do any
more than that.'

Toby was silent. He wanted to live more than
anything else, but knew Mrs Angel and Humbert were
lying. He wasn't sure whether the Kybion knew it.

Without warning, it jabbed a spiked finger at Toby.
'I will select you. I shall administer a longevity process
that will increase your life span. The others will die.'

'No!' Toby found himself protesting against his
better judgement. 'How could you expect me to help
you if you kill the others?'

The Kybion hadn't taken that into consideration
and was silent for a few seconds.

'At least let them live their natural life spans,'
Toby suggested.

'No,' gambled Mrs Angel. 'You cannot half trust us.
We would know the clerk has longevity. There is no
reason why we should not be treated in the same way.'

The Kybion sensed the deceit in the older woman
and man but, despite its threat, was not programmed
to take life.

'I won't help you unless Tasmin is able to live for

as long as I do,' insisted Toby. 'I don't care how powerful you are.' Realising his mistake before he had finished speaking, he added, 'And Mrs Angel and Mr Humbert as well.'

'Very well,' the Kybion said eventually. 'I will administer a treatment that will slow down your ageing process. You will grow older, but at a much slower rate than is natural. You will not be able to carry on your normal lives. Those who know you must believe that you are dead.' Humbert winced at the thought of having to give up his insurance money, and was soon plotting some way round it. 'I will be watching you.'

'What is it you want me to do?' Toby inquired, half afraid of the answer.

'You shall carry a small transmitter that will draw the Star Dancer to you. The planet it threatens recorded its energy pattern and they devised a signal to attract it. The transmitter was going to be installed in a fixed position but, over the passing years, the human species could dig up the unit or build over it. I cannot carry the device because the power in my circuits would disrupt its signal.' The Kybion detected that Toby was having severe doubts. 'It will not harm you, and it is unlikely the Star Dancer would. If you do this, you will save a whole species of creatures like yourself from extinction.'

'I suppose if I should be dead anyway... I've nothing to lose.' Toby was no longer sure which was the better arrangement. 'What will happen when I do meet this "Star Dancer"?'

'Do not worry. I will be here.' The Kybion turned to the others. 'I will always be here. You three will carry markers; ones that will let me know where you are at all times to ensure that you do nothing to subvert future events. Your lives must now be spent unobtrusively, for neither power, nor gain.'

Toby's conscience overwhelmed his terror, and he gave in. 'All right. I'll do it. Where will I carry this trans... mitter then? How big is it? What happens when I'm not wearing pockets?'

'You will not need pockets. There are many cavities inside your body into which it will fit quite easily.'

Toby almost fainted. The Kybion was unaware of the fear any surgical procedure held for a Victorian, otherwise it might have explained it would be totally painless.

The others certainly showed no signs of discomfort when it gave them their longevity treatment that consisted of nothing more than impregnating the skin with a needle. The process was quick. To Toby it felt like hours. The machine may have been incomplete, yet had sense enough not to let the three realise how it had fitted the tracking devices. Each marker was minute and would cling to their skeletons for as long as they lived - and after.

Tasmin, Mrs Angel, and Mr Humbert were completely re-costumed from a wardrobe in a cavity behind one of the chamber walls. At any other time it would have seemed a strange facility for a machine to have, but even Mr Humbert no longer felt inclined to question the Kybion about its odd behaviour in case it changed its metal mind. They were also handed enough to cash and bonds to ensure they could invest well and idle the years away in luxury. The Kybion's more comprehensive understanding of human nature would come later - when it was too late.

'Be brave, Toby. I'm sure we'll meet again,' Tasmin told him.

Even that affectionate reassurance couldn't revive his good humour. The clerk's life, prospects, and worldview were about to change forever.

'Take care of him,' Mrs Angel told the Kybion

imperiously, having to acknowledge that the ledger clerk had saved their lives. 'Remember that his intelligence is no more than matches his station.'

The machine hadn't a clue what she meant, so Tasmin added, 'Don't hurt him.'

'Let us out of here,' Mr Humbert demanded impatiently.

Toby found the presence of mind to give Tasmin a self-conscious hug.

Mrs Angel quickly parted them. 'Remember your vow, my girl,' she chided with consummate bad timing.

'There is a tunnel running under these cliffs. It leads to the nearest town,' said the Kybion. 'Remember, wherever you are, I will always know.'

With that warning ringing in their ears, they hastened away to freedom and new lives.

Apparently unconcerned whether they reached the other end of the dimly lit tunnel or not, the Kybion returned to the trembling Toby who was desperately wishing he had been able to go with them. The ledger clerk couldn't believe what was happening to him. The more he thought about it, the more his senses became numbed, until the clammy air and prospect of what was about to occur made him faint away.

CHAPTER 4

The urban brick and Tarmac receded and the train sped through the June countryside of velvet-green fields rippling with new corn. Gabrielle gave a deep sigh of relief. She felt better already. The bright lights and candyfloss company of her student friends would have just made her worse, and probably diabetic. Too many exams and too much study and had frayed her usually resilient composure.

Out here it was possible to see things with a clear perspective that would enable her to unwind. Gabrielle was confident of passes for every paper she had sat over the last two months, and probably wouldn't have worried too much if she weren't. Not many orphans had her assured future. Not many children grew up to retain the intense confidence of adolescence once they learnt what life was really like. There was something else making the teenager restless.

Gabrielle was a strong, healthy girl, and had overcome the severe injuries from the car crash that had killed her parents when she was four. No next of kin could be found, even in India, their homeland, but she didn't regret being put into a children's home. They had been very indulgent, and her foster parents over the past nine years had doted on the precocious and demanding girl. They knew that the child was exceptional. Although not particularly pretty, her looks were striking and expression thoughtful, as if she were always pondering something, and her eyes intelligent enough to belong to a woman twice her age.

Smuggler's Halt, the small community that had built up around the railway station, was just remote enough, without a road on the way to anywhere interesting.

As Gabrielle walked down the path to Smuggler's Row, the terrace of cottages where her foster father's sister lived, she watched the swifts and seagulls circling over the cliffs. The air carried the smell of seaweed and fumes of a bonfire.

Gabrielle was fond of her foster Aunt, Penny, and her ten-year-old daughter Paula, and almost regretted that they would be taking a morning train to go on a holiday of their own. Everyone she knew thought the student had been mad to want to live in her aunt's cottage without company for over three weeks. Gabrielle had never seen the place before, yet inexplicably knew that this was where she needed to be. The door opened as she entered the front garden

and the pixie like face of Paula beamed a mischievous
welcome.

'It is remote here,' Penny told her as she poured
the tea with one hand and rapped Paula's knuckles
with the other when she tried to sneak another piece of
fruitcake. 'But with the train and the occasional bus
you can get almost anywhere. Even walk to the village
if you want. It's not far up the coast path.'

Gabrielle yawned. 'I just want to rest. Doing all the
things adolescent girls should do must be tiring
enough. Trying to *avoid* doing all the things adolescent
girls are expected to do is even more tiring.'

Her aunt smiled. 'Don't waste your life away.
You're no adolescent and will be old soon enough.'
Penny was in her forties, and still attractive, so the
advice didn't ring true.

'Is there a library in the village?' Gabrielle asked
suddenly, as though remembering the reason she was
there.

Penny wondered if her foster niece had really
turned into the swot her brother and his wife proudly
claimed. 'A small one. The main library is in town. I've
got tickets for both.' She went to her handbag and
pulled two cards from her purse and handed them to
Gabrielle. Why shouldn't the girl study? If Penny had
possessed half her brains she would have probably
done the same when she had the chance.

'Thanks a lot. I might take a walk into the village
tomorrow.'

'Good idea. We'll need to be off early, so you'll have
all of the day to yourself.'

Gabrielle spent that night in fitful sleep and was
visited by the turbulent dreams that had haunted her
for as long as she could remember. They had become
worse with the exams. She had hoped they would
subside with some peace and quiet.

The next morning Gabrielle saw Penny and Paula

onto the train then returned to the cottage to unpack a pair of stout walking shoes from her suitcase.

It was threatening rain as she strode out over the glistening shingle, untouched by holidaymakers' feet. Walking on the pebbles was tiring, so she climbed some crumbling steps braced by railway sleepers and continued along the top of the cliff. The only other people she saw were a plump woman being taken for a walk by her dog, and the motionless figure of a fair-haired man watching her intently from a distance.

'Good morning,' said the dog owner.

It took Gabrielle a moment to realise that people out here were more relaxed about talking to strangers. 'Good morning. Looks like rain.'

'At least there's no wind. Even the seagulls hide when it blows through Wrecker's Cove.'

Gabrielle indicated the man watching them. 'He'll get soaked without a coat.'

The woman laughed. 'Oh him. He's always out here watching for something. It's about time he found what he was looking for after all these years.'

In the village library, Gabrielle found a volume on 18th century politics. It was in good condition, and last withdrawn by a researcher nine months ago. The librarian cast her a glance of admiration as she checked it out.

The student's striking looks and billowing black hair soon caught the attention of the locals, as though an Indian girl in mackintosh and walking brogues was a novelty in those parts. Curious to know more about her, some people went out of their way to be friendly, while others kept their distance. This was a world away from the brash melting pot of college campus and home.

Not wanting to appear stand-offish, Gabrielle managed to supply them with enough information about her to satisfy their curiosity and, in an attempt to show interest in their small world, enquired about the man who spent so much time standing on top of the cliff. Two older women she had struck up a conversation with smiled, secretly flattered by the attention of the well-spoken young woman.

'He's been looking out for goodness knows what on top of them cliffs for as long as I can remember,' one of them said. 'And I'm seventy.'

'He doesn't look a day over forty-five though,' joined in the other. 'And my old dad said he could remember him too.'

'Mind you, Dot,' the other woman reminded her, 'your old dad's brain did go eventually. My Ma reckoned it was his father he saw.'

'Might have been, but I don't remember his funeral. I've been to the funeral of everyone who died around here, and I can't remember him ever dying.'

Whatever the vagaries of the two women's memories, Gabrielle's curiosity had been fired. She could picture the man watching on the cliff above the village as she stood chatting. He hadn't appeared to be very old, and she wanted to know how a seventy-year-old could look no more than forty-five. 'Why doesn't somebody ask him?'

The two women were silent for a moment.

'It probably hasn't occurred to them,' Dot said.

'He never gets near enough to anyone to let them,' her companion added. 'Even his groceries are put on his back doorstep where he leaves a cheque and list for the next week.'

'You going to ask him then, dear?' Dot suggested, half in humour and half in hope.

'I could do.'

'He'll run off before you can, but I wouldn't stop you trying. A sturdy girl like you could probably catch him.' At that, Dot and her friend fell about laughing.

Gabrielle took the opportunity to escape, and made

her way to the top of the cliff where her quarry still stood. Although she hadn't really intended to, the teenager felt compelled to speak to the strange figure. Even from fifty yards away, she could feel his pale grey eyes observing her determined approach. He didn't run off as the women had suggested, and remained stock-still.

As she came closer, Gabrielle sensed the coldness of the man's penetrating gaze. His hair was fair, nearly white, and his skin wan. It was difficult to believe this face belonged to a man of forty-five, let alone seventy. His features were unlined, and a polo-necked sweater concealed his neck where telltale signs of ageing could usually be found.

'Good morning,' Gabrielle said cheerfully.

The expression in the pale eyes became suspicious, if not hostile. 'Go away.'

Despite his frosty response, she remarked in spite of herself, 'Why, you're not that old at all.'

'Go away,' he repeated then turned on his heels and almost ran from the edge of the cliff towards a flat-roofed bungalow nestling in a gully.

That should have been enough to convince Gabrielle he didn't want to hold a conversation. However, there was something so magnetic about the mysterious stranger she couldn't resist following him down the slope. He stood in the porch of the bungalow watching her approach.

She called out before getting too close and scaring him inside, 'What's the matter? I didn't mean to alarm you.'

'You didn't. Who sent you?'

Encouraged by the odd question, Gabrielle walked down to him. 'Why, nobody. I was only trying to be sociable.'

'No one round here tries to be sociable with me,' he retorted flatly. 'Are you sure no one sent you?'

'Of course they didn't. I only arrived here yesterday. Why should anyone have sent me?'

He replied with a cool, accusing look.

'The truth is,' Gabrielle admitted, 'two women in the village were trying to kid me you were seventy, and I didn't believe them.'

'You are right, I am not seventy.'

'I can see that now. Don't you let anyone talk to you?'

'Not if I can avoid it. You aren't English?'

It almost sounded like an accusation. 'Yes, I am. My parents were Indian, but I was born here. I can't remember them. I was brought up in a children's home. I couldn't even pronounce my own name if you were to ask me.' What on earth made her tell him all that when he would admit to nothing? She was usually good at mind games. Something else was going on here.

'What are you called now?'

'Gabrielle. What's your name?'

'Never you mind,' he said firmly enough for her not to ask again.

Gabrielle was unable to make him out. 'You're an odd sort of person. I'll leave you alone if that's what you want.'

The man said nothing. It was obvious his frosty manner didn't intimidate the eighteen-year-old as it did other people. As she walked back to the cliff path, his gaze followed her. There was a tinge of fear in the tight expression.

CHAPTER 5

That night Gabrielle quickly fell asleep and didn't have any dreams vivid enough to disturb her. The next morning she woke early and lay in bed looking out at the gulls circling over the cliffs. Random thoughts flowed through her mind.

Still drowsy, Gabrielle noticed the ghostly figure of a young man standing by the bedroom window. He was slightly built and had a friendly, mobile expression. Strangest of all, he was wearing nineteenth-century clothes; a frock coat and trousers that were almost threadbare and chisel-toed shoes that had all but lost their original shape. By comparison, his frilled cream shirt, which was set off by a faded maroon waistcoat, looked quite expensive. He was hatless and his smiling face seemed to sit on a wide cravat tied with meticulous care.

Gabrielle lay watching the apparition, wondering what part of her fancy had conjured him up. He pulled a newspaper called *The Daily Bugle* from under his arm. When he held it out towards her, she could see the date. There was something peculiar about it. History was Gabrielle's strongest subject; though he was obviously Victorian, the date of the paper was 1st, April 1917. Her overloaded mind must have been playing practical jokes. Feeling ridiculous, she sat upright to make sure she had only been dreaming.

All through breakfast, Gabrielle couldn't help smiling to herself about the unlikely visitor and his wrongly dated newspaper, and then started to wonder whether *The Daily Bugle* ever existed. As she showered and idly sorted out what clothes to wear, a forceful urge to go to the town library and find out struck her. There was a bus in fifteen minutes. She finished dressing and dashed out, combing her long hair on the way to the bus stop.

Gabrielle told herself she was mad to travel eight miles on a silly whim like this; but the buses were infrequent, and the trains didn't pass through the town, so she would have had to fight back her curiosity for two hours before another opportunity arose.

Gabrielle didn't need to consult her map. She had been given specific directions to every place of importance by her fellow bus passengers, happy to encourage visitors to explore the nooks and crannies of their town. The area had never been a great tourist attraction. It lacked the places of amusement and architectural splendour other resorts possessed.

The library was still housed in its Victorian monument dedicated to the education of the lower orders and, despite the unobtrusive PC stations and electronic databases, had not allowed its shelves of books to be decimated to pay for them. This library either had a private sponsor or managed to vanish from the cost cuts of the county council. This was Gabrielle's hands-on sort of place. She preferred the musty smell of old book to electronically generated pages that stunned the optic nerves and turned the concentration to mush.

The listed building had the faint aroma of disinfectant and the austere silence due it. Gabrielle felt her muscles tense as she noticed for the first time that her new shoes squeaked.

Being able to request a specific paper with an exact date meant the librarian didn't have to ask her embarrassing questions about what she was looking for. This was just as well, because she wasn't sure herself. Gabrielle was amazed to learn there was once a local paper called *The Daily Bugle,* and not only that, it hadn't yet been stored in the vaults of the town hall, also Victorian and already filled to capacity. The trainee librarian scanning records into electronic format had only got up to *The County News* before taking leave to have twins.

The 1st of April 1917 was apparently a Sunday, so Gabrielle was brought the next day's edition. Something at the back of her mind said that a date as ordinary as the 2nd of April would have easily been forgotten. It seemed that the apparition had an uncanny reasoning about it. She could feel her hands shaking as she took the newspaper in its Perspex cover. This was getting too eerie. The student thanked the librarian and carried it to a stand where she carefully turned the discoloured pages, scouring every last detail.

Reaching page five, Gabrielle was unable to believe her eyes and gave a small gasp. The man reading opposite glanced up to give her a concerned look. Under the heading of 'Man proves he is sixty-seven years old. Court upholds decision he is not eligible for conscription', was a picture of the subject, who couldn't have been over twenty-five. Then the cold, clammy truth dawned. It was, without a doubt, the face of the stranger she had accosted on the cliffs. His name was Alfred Tobias Wendle.

Stunned at the discovery, Gabrielle quickly glanced through the rest of the paper. She had a rational, thorough mind and would have cursed herself for missing something else of importance. Then she took the paper to the photocopier to make a record of the front cover and the article. This was where a little technology would have come in handy. The machine swallowed four coins before printing anything reasonably like the original. Gabrielle put its malfunctioning down to the fact it must have been Victorian as well and didn't bother to ask for her money to be refunded. She was in too much of a hurry to catch the bus back to grieve over forty pence.

There had to be an explanation for the picture. As Dot had suggested, he could have been the man's

father. Gabrielle doubted it. It was unlikely a face
would have inherited the same features so exactly.
There was only one thing for it. She must confront him
again. After yesterday's encounter it might not have
been a very promising idea, but it was either doing
that or forgetting she had ever met him.

As Gabrielle changed into her walking brogues,
she wondered about the ghostly Victorian who had
presented the paper to her. Who on earth was he?

When she reached the cliff top, her quarry was
nowhere to be seen, so she went down to the bungalow
and knocked resolutely on the door, half expecting a
bucket of water to be tipped over her head from the flat
roof.

To her surprise, a voice from inside called out,
'Come in. The door is open.'

It was his voice all right; cool, without any trace of
cordiality.

She went inside, through a small hall, and into a
large room. Everything was immaculately tidy; even
the man in the polo-neck sweater sitting at the table
over a mug of coffee was groomed like a schoolmaster
supervising an exam.

'Do you take sugar in coffee?' Wendle asked.

Gabrielle nodded.

He added a large spoonful to another steaming
mug. 'You can come in and sit down if you like.
Standing around like that looks untidy.'

'You like everything tidy?'

'I have a very tidy mind. The curse of the Victorian
clerk.'

Gabrielle sat in the chair facing him, clutching the
photocopies she had taken that morning. 'How old are
you?'

'One hundred and twenty-seven,' he replied, not
moving his gaze to ensure he didn't miss her reaction.

She half believed him. 'You've worn well.'

'It's not a blessing.' He paused. 'How much are you capable of believing?'

'How much do you want to tell me?'

'I cannot tell you part of the truth. I must tell you everything. I am not good at talking to other people. It is unlikely they would believe anything I have to say.'

'People in the village think there's something strange about you. Why not confirm their suspicions?'

'Because people will only believe what they have been taught is plausible. What is out of their experience becomes impossible.'

'I was going to ask you about this.' Gabrielle put the photocopies on the table. 'You seem to have anticipated me.'

'I was a young man once. Quite a lively good-natured fellow in a naive way. I was an impoverished ledger clerk, and wore the same suit and shoes for years. The only new garment I was able to afford for a long while was a frilled cream-coloured shirt.'

'What was his name?'

'He was called Toby?'

'Alfred Tobias Wendle?'

'Yes.'

'Then you are Toby.'

'No,' he said sharply. 'Don't call me that.' He rose abruptly and went to the window.

'Why did you want me to know about this after you've kept everything to yourself for so long?' Gabrielle enquired carefully.

Wendle gazed out at the sky. 'Because you may be intelligent enough to believe me.'

'And?' prompted Gabrielle.

'Now there is a problem. I believe I could carry on growing old at this tortuously slow rate if I can't find someone to help me.' Wendle turned and saw her puzzled expression. 'Longevity is not the marvellous thing it is made out to be by those who have never

known it. It is a living death. Though your brain
hardly ages, it becomes tired of the same old thoughts.
Nature designed the human mind to have a certain
span. You have to sleep for days at a time to escape the
boredom of it. Your real self has to escape from the
body for fear of going mad.'

'So that's who Toby is?'

'I hardly know him.'

'Why aren't you able to age at the same rate as
everyone else?'

Wendle returned to the table and sat facing
Gabrielle again. He gave her one last long look as
though to reassure himself he wasn't making a
mistake. 'I made a commitment that I would never tell
this to a living soul. I now believe that the party I
made the pledge to is not keeping to its side of the
agreement. If I am right, I must tell someone.'

Gabrielle listened to his extraordinary tale in
silence, her rational mind astounded at what it heard.
It was difficult to take in. A planet on the other side of
the Galaxy, an energy vampire called the Star Dancer
and a faceless robot capable of doubling human life
spans? It was obvious Wendle was no practical joker.
Both fascinated and alienated by him at the same
time, Gabrielle was totally convinced of his integrity.
Behind his brittle exterior there was a vulnerable
creature she was willing to help. Perhaps the greatest
assistance she could provide, though, was not to think
him mad.

Gabrielle made the formidable mental leap and
decided to believe him. 'Can I help?'

'Probably not.'

'I would if you'd let me.'

'There is nothing you can do.'

'Why not?'

'The other three, Tasmin, Humbert, and Mrs Angel
contacted me recently. They had somehow managed to

remove the markers the Kybion had impregnated them with to keep track of their movements. This enabled them to amass fortunes; Mr Humbert by collecting ship insurances and Mrs Angel and Tasmin by setting themselves up as mediums again. I believe Tasmin was always a genuine physic, yet can no longer be the woman I knew.'

'You were fond of her?'

Wendle ignored the question. 'They were not content with the fortunes the Kybion had enabled them to make, and knew I was being used to attract an energy source of immense power. What could be more profitable nowadays, than energy?'

'But if even you don't know what form it takes, how on earth will they manage to control it? If a highly advanced race on another planet can't deal with it, how could they hope to?'

'Greed can make people blind to the obvious. I am not afraid of losing my life: I am afraid of what they might try and do if they were ever to meet this Star Dancer. They could well prevent the Kybion intercepting it, and let it loose on this planet as well.'

'Then the Kybion must be warned.'

'If I knew where to find the machine, it would be. It should have contacted me a long while ago, when the Star Dancer was due to arrive. I haven't seen either of them. I'm afraid of being left like this, but dread what could happen to this other planet. I have only one advantage.'

'What's that?'

'You believe me. Even if you aren't able to help me find the Kybion, it's a relief someone else now knows.'

Gabrielle was puzzled. 'Why don't the other three have the same problem with longevity as you do?'

'Because they have materialistic minds and are now able to move about as much as they want. If I were to travel from this area, the transmitter is bound

to encounter interference that would stop it
functioning.'

'Perhaps that's happened already, and is why the
Kybion hasn't been able to contact you.'

'The Kybion was incomplete when I first met it.
That was long ago. It must have overcome that
problem by now. And I would feel it if the transmitter
stopped. If Humbert or the other two were to try and
move me from this place, I don't know what would
happen. I only know it would not be pleasant.'

'At least they wouldn't get the Star Dancer.' She
could see he wasn't impressed. 'Yes. I suppose that
could be pretty disastrous as well.'

'Especially if they tried to cut the transmitter out
of me. At least, I wouldn't be very happy about it.'

'Don't suppose the police would be any use?'
Wendle gave her an even cooler look. 'No, they
wouldn't believe even part of it. There's only one thing
for it then.'

'What's that?'

'Toby will have to let me know if anything happens
to you.'

'No!' Wendle snapped.

'Why not? The other three aren't able to conjure up
alter egos in the same way, are they? Even your
Tasmin doesn't have that ability, does she?'

'It's unlikely.'

'Then they can't find out what we're up to, can
they?'

'Not as far as I know. But I did not intend you to
take any risks.'

'Who says I will?' Gabrielle replied innocently.

Wendle paused for a moment, and then seemed
satisfied. He poured out two more mugs of coffee. They
sat in silence drinking until the grandfather clock
struck. It looked oddly out of place in the uncluttered
room. The hollow chime urged Gabrielle to move.

Obediently she gathered up the photocopies and her shoulder bag, and left with a brief farewell to the preoccupied Wendle.

That night she slept unusually deeply. Her subconscious needed time to digest the revelations before the next strange day arrived.

Wendle remained seated at the table in his bungalow, not daring to fall asleep. He heard the breeze catch the kitchen window and blow it open but he was too exhausted to go and close it. If he had been his usual vigilant self, he would have sensed the figure standing behind him.

A quick hand pressed a pad over his nose and mouth. After a brief violent struggle, all the cool breezes of the Channel couldn't have roused him.

CHAPTER 6

With a sharp crack, the screen measuring the level in the energy pool shattered. Opu didn't turn to see how it had happened. She was busy keeping the power as constant as possible. It was either that or shutting down another refractor, and with five other stations out of commission that wouldn't have been a good idea. Everyone's consumption had already been rationed and the energy giving yellow sun was about to enter its short phase. By the time it was at its regular meridian again, it could well be shining down on a world minus intelligent life.

'Damn evolution,' swore Opu. 'Why the heck can't we go without perpetual nourishment, like our ancestors?'

There was a familiar voice from the balcony. 'Can't invent anything to shift us back in time.'

'Come inside, Annac. You might as well be in here as anywhere else when we all drop out like spent meteors, one by one, round the globe.'

Annac joined the harassed controller-in-charge.
'Your little plan not working, eh?'

'You invented the system. What went wrong?'

'Did it arrive there?'

'So Taigal Rax says.'

'Then my end went all right. Must have been your machine or the fancy bits they added to it.'

'But it must have worked,' insisted Opu. 'It was faultless. It was repeatedly checked.'

'Has the Kybion contacted them?' asked Annac.

'Not yet. They can't raise it.'

'Then they must have given it a mind of its own. After all, we don't understand enough about the creatures on the Star Dancer's planet to know what idiosyncrasies it needed.'

'The Kybion may have become faulty.'

'Don't let it cross your mind.'

'The thought has been trampling through my mind ever since we should have been receiving results.'

'You need a short break.'

'You must be joking.'

'Believe me,' said Annac, 'I did a permanent shift when those solar flares shattered eleven refractors and, if I hadn't taken a short break, I wouldn't have thought my way out of it. Don't worry, the problem will still be here when you come back. You could go and see your youngster if you want.'

'*That* I would not survive at the present time.'

'If you don't change your mind about that child soon, it could grow up with a complex.'

'If that bundle of circuits and crystals doesn't do something about this Star Dancer soon, nobody will have the chance to grow up.'

'Still, I want you to meet someone.'

'Oh?'

'It's not far. Looks as though the Star Dancer is through with you for this shift anyway.' She pointed to the remains of the energy level.

Opu saw that it was still and sighed with relief. She handed over to another controller and went to the balcony with Annac.

'Where to?' Opu asked.

'Just follow me.'

'Well, don't swerve about, will you. My reflexes aren't up to avoiding mid-air collisions.'

'My wings are as steady as they ever were,' Annac assured her with the arrogance of old age, and lurched from the balcony into the air.

Many near collisions later, Annac and Opu were circling over an untidy clutter of spherical homes. They had become stacked, higgledy-piggledy on top of each other over thousands of years and looked an eyesore from the air. Some were so old no one bothered to demolish them because they thought it was only a matter of time before they fell down of their own accord.

Annac spiralled towards one of the lowest in the stack and Opu followed at a safe distance. Alighting on a narrow balcony and passing through a curtain of light beams, they found themselves in a large round room littered with antique apparatus.

'Hey,' Annac called to a recess, 'don't you know there's an emergency on?'

'Then how did you manage to find time to come here?' came back a voice. 'I always thought your input was so invaluable - unlike us poor seers.'

'Because I've come to consult a seer,' Annac shouted back, and in so doing woke a lounging figure who rolled over onto her back, crumpling a wing. 'What a way to spend an emergency,' commented the old Ojalie contemptuously.

'I was trying to conserve energy until you lit in here like a miracle from the moon,' retorted the recumbent visitor. 'I'm very energy conscious at the moment.'

'Aren't we all,' agreed Opu wryly.

'Come on Anaru,' called Annac. 'We haven't got all this sun. It was your idea after all.'

'I've just finished setting it up,' Anaru flitted from the alcove. She immediately threw her arms about Opu in greeting and completely ignored Annac. 'I'm sure it might help if we give it a chance,' she bubbled. 'Now everyone clear the loop please.' She ushered her reclining guest out. 'We need all the room we can get for this.'

Opu recognised the equipment. 'But this is an old-fashioned mental loop.'

'That's right! That's right!' Anaru fluttered her wings in excitement. 'And you'll never guess who I got through to only a short while ago?'

'Who?' asked Opu, just managing to be polite.

'The Water Planet.'

'She means Taigal Rax,' Annac explained.

Opu had already guessed that. 'We are able to contact them at the speed of thought, you know,' Opu reminded her.

'Ah,' Anaru lifted a stubby finger, 'but are you able to contact the planet where the Kybion is?'

'Of course not. If the android built a receiver that powerful, it would be more than a little conspicuous. At the moment the wretched thing won't even contact Taigal Rax.'

'But what if you *could* contact it?'

'The Kybion is a machine; it doesn't have a mental link you can raise.'

'But humans have!'

'Oh no, I've got all the problems I need for one lifetime.'

'Why not?' asked Annac, who hadn't been known for flights of fancy.

'This is an evolving species. Even if we could

contact these humans, it's unlikely they would understand us.'

'Is that what they call themselves?' asked Annac.

'Apparently.'

'We're still evolving. Any species that isn't is an extinct one.'

'If we make a bad contact we can easily break off,' Anaru insisted. 'We only have to shut down the power. Let me show you how it works.' Opu lowered her beak in disapproval. 'Please...'

'Oh, all right,' Opu said somewhat disagreeably.

Anaru was already connecting the equipment before the words were out of her mouth. 'I'll just let them know I'm coming through.' She dashed into the alcove.

'Hey,' called Opu, 'that's cheating.' She turned on Annac. 'How did she manage to get a link into the computer signal?'

'Stop complaining, it doesn't make any difference to your transmissions.'

'Get on with it then,' Opu snapped as Anaru reappeared.

'Now don't rush me,' the seer protested. 'I must concentrate.' She sat upright on the floor with her wings outspread, looking like an ancient statuette. 'Don't interrupt, and look at the screen.'

Annac and Opu joined her on the floor and did as she said. With a beam of power playing about her broad skull, Anaru's thoughts were projected onto the frequency selected on the screen. Within seconds, an image began to flicker before them. The distinct features of an aquatic Taigalian appeared.

'You can speak to her if you become part of the loop,' Anaru told Opu. 'There'll be no language problem as long as you don't move out of it.'

Unexpectedly impressed, Opu moved into the loop and studied the amphibious features on the screen.

They were shimmering silver and framed with white-edged scales. Double lids protected the eyes, and a nostril in the centre of the forehead occasionally opened and closed.

'My name is Controller Opu,' she thought.

The response was immediate. 'I am Healphani-Kioyono. I know of you, but am not connected with the transmission of the Kybion. We hope your problem is resolved soon.'

'So do I,' Opu absently thought. It was instantly transmitted across the Galaxy.

'Anaru told us she would like to link with the planet, Perimeter 84926. If you permit it, I can find out the co-ordinates of the Kybion. She may be able to pick up a human sensitive in its vicinity.'

'As long as it doesn't interfere with its function, anything's worth trying.' Opu was becoming more impressed by the minute. 'Though all official contact will be made through my control.'

'Of course. This is purely experimental. We could boost Anaru's signal should she need it.'

'We must conserve the power now, Healphani. Reception's getting erratic,' Anaru cut in. 'Many thanks. I'll be back to you as soon as I can.' She slapped the disc that shut down the equipment.

'Well?' said Annac.

It was obvious Opu had changed her mind about seers. 'Yes,' she admitted. 'You're not often wrong.' Then she turned to Anaru. 'Even if you can reach a human on that planet, how will you make them understand, let alone help us?'

'We talk through thought, so won't need a translator. It's purely a matter of selecting the right sensitive,' explained Anaru.

'Forgive me,' Opu said, 'it's my job to be sceptical. I'm not handed prizes for believing in miracles.'

Annac pulled herself up. 'I'm not surprised you had

a brat for a child,' she commented dryly. 'I'll see you later Anaru.'

Anaru fidgeted herself out of her statuesque position. 'Well, don't come back and interfere until I tell you. Your ideas have too many angles to be of any use in here. Goodbye, Opu. I hope we see each other again.'

'You're the seer. You should know whether that's going to happen,' Opu reminded her somewhat unkindly.

Anaru just chuckled and returned to her alcove.

CHAPTER 7

It was dawn when Gabrielle half woke and turned to see the familiar figure of Toby standing by the window. He was holding something out to her; an address written on a sheet of paper. Reaching for the pencil and notepad she always kept beside her bed, Gabrielle copied the words before he faded from sight.

As she shook herself awake, Gabrielle realised that his expression had been tense and unsmiling. Something was wrong. She tumbled out of bed and went to the bathroom to splash water on her face, then returned to the bedroom to read the address written on the pad. 'High Acre Grange, Haymaker's Green' it read. Wondering whether her mind was playing tricks again, she pulled out her local map. There actually was a place called Haymaker's Green.

After what he had told her, it seemed probable that Wendle had been kidnapped and taken to that address. Gabrielle had no idea what to do next. Even if she told the police, no one at the Grange was going to admit it and let them search the place without something better than her suspicion to go on.

What to do? The address was a good twelve miles away. Then she remembered Penny's bike in the backyard. It was under a primitive lean-to shed, and fortunately not padlocked.

Gabrielle snatched a quick breakfast, showered, and then dressed in jeans and T-shirt, trying to look as inconspicuous as possible. Armed with her map, she peddled furiously along the path to Wendle's bungalow.

The door was ajar, and when she entered it was obvious that a struggle had taken place. She worked out the quickest route to Haymaker's Green and jumped back onto Penny's bike.

Gabrielle cycled non-stop for those twelve miles and hardly had enough energy left to circle the wide green to find the right address. When she found it, the sight of the long drive leading to the house almost filled her with despair. And what was she going to do when she did reach the door? The only thing she could think of was to apply for a job as a scullery maid. The place looked as though it needed a large staff to keep it going. Having the sense not to go to the huge front door at the top of two flights of wide steps, she peddled over the courtyard of pale, pink granite chips to the tradesman's entrance.

Before Gabrielle could dismount, a tall black man who looked as though he must have been in charge of something crossed her path.

'Hello,' she sang out. 'Friend of mine says you need someone to work in the kitchen.'

The man's clean-shaven features were immobile for a moment as rapid thoughts, and possibly astonishment, passed behind them. Then his face lit up.

'No, no - she meant a laundry maid.'

'Oh.' Gabrielle was glad it was a cleaner job. 'Got no references.'

'That's all right. Nobody stops here long anyway. You probably won't either. When can you start?'

'Now if you want,' she told him like a diffident teenager, trying not to sound suspiciously enthusiastic.

'You're a big girl. Uniform won't fit. You'll have to borrow a black skirt from Alice, and that'll be too large... But nobody'll notice. Still, I can show you around today. Got your cards?'

'Cards?' Gabrielle queried with convincing innocence.

'Yes, young lady. And P45.' He was obviously used to the problem. 'We have to pay stamps so you can get tranquillisers on the National Health after working here for a couple of days.' Her blank expression spoke volumes. 'Oh, don't worry, I'll show you how to apply for them. Stow your bike over there and come inside.' He bounced into the staff entrance. It was just as well he never asked for her CV; she hadn't yet been to university, and it was already a little too accomplished for a laundry maid.

The servants' quarters were impressive and, in the subdued light, Gabrielle's escort looked even more imposing, or would have done if it weren't for that nonchalant bounce in his step. As he passed the occasional maid, secretary or thinly disguised guard, he greeted them with the same quick, insincere grin and flourish of the hand. By the time Gabrielle had been shown all the rooms she needed to know about, she seriously began to wonder how anybody, even a crook, could have managed to employ this unlikely, irreverent man in the patterned, satin waistcoat as a butler. Finally she was shown to a large bedroom with curtained bed, wall tapestries, and marble fireplace.

'Linen in this place will have to be changed every day,' her escort announced. 'Got a special visitor coming tomorrow. Be your first job.'

'Oh? Must be a fussy sort of geezer,' she said, angling.

'Well, I suppose surgeons are.'

Gabrielle gulped back an exclamation of horror and said instead, 'What's your name then?'

'Weatherby. What's yours?'

'Jennifer,' she answered quickly.

Weatherby looked disapprovingly down at her faded jeans, T-shirt and long, tangled hair, and pondered. 'No... You couldn't be a Jennifer.'

'No?' Gabrielle felt a cold sweat round her neck.

'Scheherazade,' he decided. 'Probably wrong continent, but old man'll like that better. Might even suit you when you're tidied up.'

'Oh...' Gabrielle sighed with relief, hoping she wouldn't have to know a thousand and one tales as well. They'd all have been about Florence Nightingale, Disraeli, and the Ming Dynasty, if she did. 'When do I have to start in the morning then?'

'Seven thirty.' Gabrielle grimaced. 'Or whenever you like. Could live in if you want. Can't be too fussy in this place. As long as things get done we aren't bothered by anyone. It's his heavy boys Mr Gunn keeps tabs on.'

'Heavy boys?' Gabrielle exclaimed.

Weatherby grinned cynically. 'We have trouble with the mice. They won't bother you. He keeps them on short leads.'

Gabrielle followed Weatherby back down the stairs, trying to remember the layout of the mansion.

'Don't suppose there's any chance of stopping here tonight is there?' she asked tentatively.

Weatherby threw a quizzical glance back over his shoulder at her.

'Only I got trouble at home y'see. Brother don't like this boy I'm seeing.'

'No problem, if that's what you want. You'll have to get your own meal today, though, if you want to eat. The cook's going through one of her emotional phases. Mr Gunn's been playing her up something awful and she's a bit sensitive at the moment.'

'Oh thanks. And I don't mind where I sleep.' But Weatherby had bounced too far ahead to hear.

In the large kitchen Gabrielle was introduced to the emotional cook. The delicate frills of her blouse sleeves and collar beneath the white overall, and the heavy mesh stockings clung awkwardly to the contours of a very solid-boned frame.

'Call me Alice,' the cook said in a husky voice, reaching out to take Gabrielle's hand.

'Her real name's Arthur, but call her Alice,' Weatherby quipped.

The cook cast him a warning glance. 'Don't pay any attention to him, my dear. Because this place finds it difficult to keep staff it attracts all sorts of riffraff. Though it's not surprising. You've no idea what a dreadful man Mr Gunn can be.'

'That's right,' said Weatherby, 'now she'll really want to stay.' He turned to Gabrielle. 'Just how serious is this problem with your brother?'

Alice turned on him. 'It wouldn't hurt you to do the laundry once in a while. You're always interfering in everyone else's jobs.'

'I'm paid to. I am the head butler.'

Alice sneered. 'Head butler indeed. You're the only butler who's ever been here since you rolled up three month ago.'

'Four.'

'Is Mr Gunn really that bad?' interrupted Gabrielle before Alice could get really worked up.

'Only if you meet him,' Weatherby said reassuringly.

'I won't need to, will I?'

'Oh, you shouldn't worry,' Alice told her. 'He'll like a handsome young thing like you. Only don't go and make the mistake of throwing up the first time you set eyes on his face.'

Gabrielle's eyebrows must have risen sufficiently for Weatherby to explain, 'Mr Gunn's facial attributes are not all that attractive.'

'He's grotesque,' Alice declared.

This certainly sounded like the Mr Humbert Wendle had described, and the house and guards could have easily concealed a prisoner without anyone else knowing.

Gabrielle only met two part-time housekeepers, a handyman, two gardeners, and a kitchen maid, and wondered how they managed to maintain the place by themselves. She also discovered that Mr Gunn's bodyguards were the only ones allowed near him. They even escorted an older woman and her companion who were visiting Mr Gunn that afternoon.

The next day Gabrielle managed to busy herself convincingly by running backwards and forwards along the long landing that overlooked the main hall carrying bundles of laundry. Most of it went into the huge washing machines and was hung on lines in the back yard. She helped one of the housekeepers with the ironing then made the beds.

Although quite exhausted by the evening, Gabrielle had noticed the much used door to a lower floor opening and closing automatically to let the guards pass through. Because she could only see the tops of heads from the landing, one of them might have been Mr Gunn for all she knew. Gabrielle had better sense than to arouse suspicion by asking what was down there and waited until the place was quite deserted.

Being the new girl, she found it difficult to break away from the gossip in the kitchen. Inventing an elaborate family saga to back up the story about her bully of a brother was more taxing than putting the cover on a king-size duvet. When she eventually managed to break free, she was at least sure where everyone else was.

Gabrielle knew that there must have been an easier way to get down to the lower floor than through that automatic door, and wandered round the pink gravelled backyard looking for an outside entrance. She carefully picked her way round the house in the slowly descending summer dusk. As though he had read her thoughts, a familiar shape stood waiting for her by an ivy-covered alcove beneath some large windows. Toby pointed down. At first she could only see the blanket of ivy. He remained resolutely where he was, so she pushed the tangle of leaves with her foot.

There was a door under the ivy. With a hollow crack, the rotten wood fell from its hinges and crashed down a short flight of steps. Gabrielle froze at the noise, sure she would be discovered. There was nothing else for it but to flee down the steps after it. She fought her way through the ivy, pulled it back after her to cover the entrance, and then waited a few moments to make sure she hadn't attracted attention. When nobody came out to investigate, she groped her away along the rough wall at the bottom of the steps.

As her eyes became accustomed to the dark, Gabrielle realised she was in an ancient coal cellar. She didn't need a degree in ancient buildings to know that if she reached up she would find the slanting doors that should have been on the outside of the coal cellar. But that was wrong. The coal chute should have been on the outside of the house and the steps on the inside, unless it was constructed by a builder with a grudge against the owner. On the opposite side of the cellar, Gabrielle found the coal chute above a pile of ancient coke from a century old delivery. She carefully climbed on to it in the gloom and gingerly reached up to push the doors open. It led to a tiled pathway lit by skylights in the top of a wall. The extension had been

built over the demolished remains of another building
and part of its garden. She nearly tripped over stacks
of ancient flowerpots that had been left there.

Although she could now see where she was going,
Gabrielle didn't know which way to turn. Then Toby
reappeared. He led her along the enclosed tiled garden
path until they came to a rusty grating at a dead end.
It was possible to see through into a dimly lit corridor
below. It was long and quite deserted. Not thinking for
one moment that she could wrench the grating out
with her bare hands, Gabrielle half-heartedly shook it.
To her amazement it came free. This was too much of a
coincidence and she turned to look accusingly at Toby,
but his fancy cream shirt and fading frock coat were
nowhere to be seen.

Things were going too well for Gabrielle's rational
mind. The very fact that she was able to get this far so
easily made her suspicious when anyone else would
have put it down to luck. She pushed her way through
the hole and lowered herself down.

Although it was below ground, the air felt warm
and dry, and there was the faint whirr of an air
conditioning fan. Gabrielle moved cautiously up the
corridor. The door at the end of it opened without
difficulty. Someone had very conveniently forgotten to
secure the heavy bolt on the other side. Ahead was the
motionless figure of Toby waiting for her to catch up.
He must have been the one making her progress so
easy, yet how could a ghost draw back a bolt or loosen
a grating?

Gabrielle hesitated for a moment. Was someone
expecting her? Gunn could only know that Wendle had
spoken to her if he'd told him. It wasn't possible, she
decided, and followed Toby once more. He stopped by a
grille at the bottom of the wall. She looked down into a
white-walled room. Inside were four men. Two were
guarding a door, and an obese figure was standing over

someone lying on a table. It was Wendle. From the grotesque, bloated features of the man by him, it was easy to deduce that this was Mr Gunn. He was frantically trying to wake Wendle up. Gabrielle noticed that Toby was getting fainter and fainter. He vanished as Wendle was brought to his senses by Gunn's hefty smack to his face.

'At last,' Gunn growled. 'Don't think you can get out of this by staying unconscious forever. I'm not going to have you killed just yet.'

'Why not?' murmured Wendle, 'Haven't you taken out any insurance on me?'

Gunn clearly didn't like this accurate reference to his method of amassing a fortune, and hit out again. By this time Wendle was fully conscious and managed to roll from the table before more damage could be done. He obviously preferred to be asleep, with or without the aid of chloroform.

'I've told you, I don't know anything about this Star Dancer,' Wendle pleaded. 'The Kybion didn't tell me any more than you already know, I swear.'

'Of course you know, you lying pup!' Gunn bellowed. 'You never did have any respect for me, but I've got too much to lose to put up with your bloody-mindedness now.'

'What's the difference if you're going to get a surgeon to remove the transmitter anyway?'

'The difference is whether you get an anaesthetic or not when he does it.'

Gabrielle could see Wendle stiffen. The nausea in the pit of her stomach told her she would have to do something before the surgeon arrived the next morning.

Gunn continued to rail at his victim like a sadistic toad for as long as his body had the breath, adding a few more threats worse than the one he had already made. Then he stormed out, leaving the two guards with Wendle. There was no way to get to him from where she was. The grille would have needed more than Toby's supernatural powers to shift it without alerting the guards. There was nothing Gabrielle could do but return to the servants' quarters before she was missed.

CHAPTER 8

Gabrielle daren't risk going to sleep for fear of the events triggering one of her terrible nightmares. The last thing she needed to do was attract attention by calling out in her sleep. So she sat at the window of her attic bedroom, waiting.

In the early hours, a car drew up in front of the house. Carefully pushing the widow open, she leaned out to listen.

'Couldn't make it sooner,' called a man as he climbed from the car.

'It's only three,' Gunn's voice came back, but not so loudly. 'Keep it quiet, can't you.' Then he told one of his guards, 'Get his case.'

'You were joking about the anaesthetic, weren't you?' the visitor asked apprehensively.

'No. He still hasn't told me anything. Don't start getting squeamish. You're being paid enough, aren't you?'

'Yes. I'm getting paid enough,' was the resigned reply of a blackmailed man.

Gabrielle didn't wait to hear any more. She had stealthily made her way down to the hall and concealed herself beneath the stairs by the time the surgeon's case had been brought in. It was impossible for her to get through the automatic doors with the men passing in and out, so she was relieved when Wendle was escorted by two henchmen from the basement and across the hall to another room.

When the hall was empty, Gabrielle was about to
make her way to the room when a familiar voice
behind her said, 'Strange how these warm nights keep
one awake, isn't it?'

She spun round in surprise. Weatherby's
mischievous smile beamed at her from the gloom.

She should have been terrified. The fright made
her furious instead, and she blurted out, 'What are you
doing, sneaking about like that?'

'You're no laundry maid. You're too grand to be a
lady-in-waiting.'

'And you're no butler!'

'Then you tell me what I'm doing, sneaking about
here.'

'How should I know?' she snapped. 'You could be a
policeman for all I care.' The smile faded. 'You are a
policeman, aren't you - I thought you were too daft to
be a butler.'

'Thanks.' Weatherby sounded genuinely
crestfallen, though it was probably all part of the act.
'And I thought I was going to get a medal out of this.'

'What is your real name then?' Gabrielle
demanded.

'Weatherby. What's yours?'

'Jennifer.'

'No, really, it *is* Weatherby.'

'You must be joking.'

He stepped into the hall light and she could see his
expression. 'You're not kidding are you? Mine's
Gabrielle. Why didn't you change your name?'

'Would have meant giving me new cover and that
could have been expensive. So, as I don't come from
these parts, it didn't matter too much. It's not as if we
thought there was anything violent going on.'

'So you don't have any backup?'

'Looks as though I've got you.'

'Don't count on it. I failed the Girl Guides.'

'So we're going to need backup?'

'Believe it.'

'For fraud?'

'You haven't a clue, have you?'

'Clueless, that's me. Matches the waistcoat.'

'Don't you know that somebody is about to be horribly murdered?'

'How horribly?'

'Oh, where's the point.' Gabrielle strode across the hall to the room where Wendle had been taken.

This took Weatherby by surprise and he darted after her.

'Now that could develop into something serious.'

'So what are you going to do about it?'

'I've got to have proof of intent at least,' he hedged. 'How can you be so sure there's going to be a murder?'

Gabrielle was tired of the game and decided to gamble. 'If you know half of what I do, then you won't need proof.' She rapped the door hard and shouted, 'Mr Humbert! I want to talk to you!'

There was a stony silence both inside and outside the room. Weatherby froze momentarily, and then sprinted back to the cover of the stairs. The door slowly opened to reveal a circle of amazed expressions. Without being invited, Gabrielle strolled inside and found herself face to face with the grotesque, puffy features of Gunn.

'Good morning, Mr Humbert,' she said coolly, realising to her own surprise that she was totally calm, 'I've heard so much about you, I thought it was time we met.'

'Who are you?' blustered Gunn, half outraged and half-afraid, 'I don't recall meeting you before?'

'Oh, we've never met. It's just that I've heard so much about you I couldn't resist finding out whether it was all true.' Gabrielle had to subdue the urge to look about the room to see where Wendle was. It would have been fatal to show any interest that could have connected them. She was in enough trouble already.

'Where did you get that name Humbert from?'

'Oh, I'm a journalist. I'm afraid I practised a little deception in applying for a job here as a laundry maid.' She paused tantalisingly. 'Not so long ago I came across some fascinating reports about ships lost at sea. And I found some pictures.'

'What ship? What pictures?' snarled Gunn, growing redder and redder.

'Of a Victorian ship, and a shipping merchant who looked remarkably like you.'

'Are you trying to blackmail me?' His small eyes squinted dangerously.

Gabrielle laughed. 'What, Mr Humbert? In front of all these people?'

'Well, you're not calling on me at this time of night just to get background for a story.'

'You are a difficult man to meet.' Gabrielle could feel the charade begin to founder like one of his insured ships.

'Him!' Gunn suddenly roared, pointing to Wendle. 'You're here because of him!'

'Who?' inquired Gabrielle innocently, and let her gaze follow his pointing finger.

When she saw Wendle's face, her coolness turned to blazing fury. He had been bruised and cut, almost beyond recognition. She should have been terrified; all she could feel was uncontrollable rage rising from the pit of her stomach.

'Get her out of here!' Gunn roared to one of his guards, who looked like a cross between the side of a house and a sewer rat.

Before he could lay a finger on her he was stopped in his ungainly tracks by a sight more alarming than an angry Gabrielle.

An explosion of fire spontaneously engulfed one of

the heavy velvet curtains and reduced it to ashes in a
split second.

'What the hell was that?' yelled one of the guards
in alarm.

'The place is on fire!' called back another with a
little more perception, 'Get an extinguisher.'

'Fire be damned!' shouted the surgeon. 'That was
an explosion! I'm getting out of here, Gunn.' He
snatched up his bag of surgical instruments and made
for the door.

Gunn took a pistol from his inside pocket. 'If
anyone tries to leave I'll kill them!'

Gabrielle wondered how Weatherby had detonated
the firebomb without being in the room. As Gunn
poured out a stream of hysterical words, she began to
understand.

'It's here!' he screamed. 'The transmitter brought it
here! Can't you see? Put him in the middle of the room
away from everyone else, you idiots, before it
incinerates all of us!'

Without knowing what Gunn was ranting about,
one of the guards seized hold of Wendle and hurled
him to the floor in the centre of the room. As the men
backed away from him, Gabrielle suspected she would
be safer with Wendle, and dashed over before anyone
could stop her.

'Get her out of here, can't you!' Gunn screamed
again.

The henchman who had tried to eject her
previously moved forward.

A column of white fire soared up through the
carpet and burned away the floor he was about to
tread on, searing his eyebrows. He ran from the room
shrieking in terror.

Weatherby immediately bounced in and enquired
innocently, 'What's the matter, Mr Gunn? I thought I
smelt burning.'

'Mind your own business, you interfering imbecile!' snapped Gunn. 'Phone Mrs Tavistock and tell her.'

'I really think we should phone the fire brigade instead, Mr Gunn,' waffled Weatherby.

'Don't argue!' Gunn cuffed the tall policeman so hard round the ear he almost knocked himself over. Weatherby just looked mildly offended and pretended to rummage through his pockets for a mobile phone.

This gave the other guards and the surgeon chance to escape from the spreading flames. When Gunn raised his pistol again, his captive audience had gone. Even he now had to admit that the room was on fire, and if he wanted to save the transmitter attracting the Star Dancer, he would have to save Wendle as well.

'Pick him up,' Gunn ordered Weatherby, waving the pistol at him. 'Bring him outside.'

Weatherby stopped looking for his mobile, made his way around the flames to Gabrielle, and took off his jacket to wrap it round Wendle's shoulders.

'It's all right,' the policeman whispered to Gabrielle. 'There's no need to worry about a thing,' and smiled in a way that confirmed her doubts about his sanity.

'Outside! Outside!' ordered Gunn.

Weatherby picked up Wendle with surprising ease.

'Keep him away from me.' Gunn backed into the hall where the rest of the staff were too busy evacuating the building to pay any attention to what he was doing.

Weatherby inexplicably faltered before he reached the main entrance as though unsure which way to turn. Another column of fire shot up before him and blocked their way.

Gunn screamed, 'Get rid of him! Get rid of him! Keep him away from me!'

'Why don't you make up your mind?' Weatherby snapped back in exasperation.

'Looks as though we're trapped!' Gabrielle called as smokeless flames surrounded them. Fires must have started simultaneously in a dozen different places.

'How soon do buildings usually burn down after you've been employed in them?' asked Weatherby.

Before she could tell him he was a prat, Gunn was taking aim at Wendle and squeezing the trigger.

'Look out!' Gabrielle dragged them both to the floor.

Gunn took aim again.

Then his body shuddered violently, as though his whole bloated being was contracting.

'What's happening?' Gabrielle gasped, but at last Weatherby was speechless.

Gunn's body shrivelled, leaving his outsize clothes hanging on him like a collapsed tent. His features shrank until there was no flesh between his skin and the skull beneath it. The creature that was once Gunn stood against the background of the burning hall for a few seconds, and then collapsed to dust that swirled about in the heat of the flames.

Gabrielle and Weatherby were aware that their situation was potentially no better. The intense smokeless flames that had been licking around the hall were now roaring and the upper floors were well alight and about to collapse. There was no window to climb out of, and even the basement was belching flames. This is what heretics experienced at the stake. At that moment the freethinking Gabrielle would have converted to anything to avoid them.

The air pressure suddenly changed and a loud noise thundered past them like a speeding train to strike the smouldering wallpaper and plaster by the front entrance. A large hole was punched through the masonry and they could see the mêlée outside.

Weatherby and Gabrielle sprinted through the gap carrying Wendle and stumbled down the steps into the waiting arms of Alice and other staff. Gunn's henchmen and the surgeon had disappeared.

Everyone sat huddled a safe distance away while the local fire crew put a filter in the nearest lily pond and tried to pump water on the blaze. Without a mains hydrant, there wasn't enough pressure for the water to reach the first storey. By the time other pumps arrived, the building was a pile of smouldering rubble, punctuated by the skeletal remains of chimney stacks.

'Never known a fire burn like that before,' Gabrielle overheard a fire officer remark to a policeman. 'Even the masonry couldn't take the heat. Seems like a fishy one to me.'

At that moment Gabrielle was just relieved to be alive, and didn't even have the energy to argue with Weatherby.

Somehow, in the anticlimax, she remembered Penny's bike and expected to find it incinerated along with everything else near the house. To her relief it had been shielded from the blaze by the corrugated zinc roof of the cycle shed. An obliging policeman crammed the bike, almost successfully, into the boot of a police car while she flopped onto the rear seat and dozed most of the way back to Smuggler's Halt. Weatherby went to hospital with Wendle and promised to let her know how he was.

At nine o'clock in the morning the phone in the hall rang. Gabrielle, who had been waiting for the call, lifted the receiver and managed to murmur the number. Weatherby sounded as sickeningly cheerful as ever. Wendle was in a much better condition than could have been expected, and was due to be discharged later that day. Gabrielle would have been surprised if she hadn't been so tired, and muttered her approval when he asked if he could bring him to the cottage so she could keep an eye on him, as he had no next of kin or friends. Weatherby had an investigation to follow up and wouldn't be free for a couple of days.

After a refreshing few hours snooze, it occurred to Gabrielle there was something odd about the conversation with Weatherby. After Gunn's death, what else could be so important that he had to dash off and investigate it? And why shouldn't Wendle be just as safe in hospital or his own bungalow? It was evident when Wendle arrived in a police car that he didn't think much of the idea either. His wits had returned with a vengeance after the night's experience, and he seemed more furious than thankful at the risk Gabrielle had taken to save him. The bruises he had sustained were now patches of unsightly discoloration on his face and his near roasting hadn't warmed up his cool manner.

Gabrielle could tell he was still worried about something. 'How much does Weatherby know about you and what started the fire?'

'He was investigating insurance frauds. For all he knows he still is,' was the stiff reply. 'I have not told him anything to make him think differently.'

'Perhaps just as well.'

'He will be coming back here to talk to you of course,' Wendle reminded her, and then suddenly added, 'Get well away from this place before he does.'

Gabrielle didn't believe her ears. 'What on earth are you talking about?'

'While you are near me you are in danger. I told you I didn't want you to take any risks.'

'Given the way things happened, I didn't have much choice!'

'You do not understand the danger you what are in, you silly little fool. Get as far away from here as you can before your luck runs out as well.'

Instead of wondering about the sudden change in Wendle, lack of proper sleep made Gabrielle unreasonable. 'Don't preach at me!' She stormed back at him, 'You're the one who got me involved in this, remember!'

'I made a mistake. I should have told you nothing.'

'Well it's a bit late now.' She marched into the kitchen to wash up the plates left over from the last two days.

'Things are going to get worse,' he called after her. 'There is nothing I can do about this Star Dancer. You saw what it was capable of last night.'

There was no reply apart from the clattering of crockery in the kitchen and the screaming of herring gulls outside.

CHAPTER 9

The six-hoofed Kyrupa galloped round and round the shattered refractor station as though they knew it was only a matter of time before they became the most intelligent species on Ojal.

In the midst of their grazing pasture of shimmering herbs, the remains of a station's domed refractor shields lay twisted and seared.

Controller-in-charge Opu had been catapulted backwards and forwards on a travel beam to survey the damage and attempt to restore the confidence of the station crews dotted about the globe. It hadn't been her first priority, but a sinister lull in the attacks of the Star Dancer meant that she could no longer avoid giving confidence-boosting pep talks. She doubted that the pause in the entity's activity was due to any success the Kybion had been having on Perimeter 84926. Taigal Rax had still heard nothing from it. The machine's competence was now in doubt: it must have been malfunctioning. That being the case, not many Ojalie would live to know the reason why.

In an attempt to prevent the Star Dancer sucking their energy pool dry, the demolished station's crew had tried to close its refractor shields. Their disagreement with the marauding entity had left them scattered in pieces about the otherwise peaceful countryside.

'Well, it was worth a try, I suppose,' Opu told the controllers, wondering how desperation could have made anyone do something so stupid. 'Looks as though you're out of commission from now on. Just as well it seems to be occupied elsewhere at the moment,' she waffled, wishing somebody would just tell her to shut up and go home.

Opu completed her survey of the operational stations, and then returned to her own Main Base Station 93. Winging her way over other Ojalies preparing to sunbathe, she needed to check its massive shields before the next onslaught.

'Couldn't be caused by a freak storm of collapsars about the size of atoms, do you think?' said a familiar voice from the top of the perilously high dome.

Opu looked up to see the furiously fluttering wings of Annac as she clung to the slippery surface.

She sighed. 'We would have picked up anything like that before it reached the edge of the solar system. And what are you doing up here? It's dangerous, even without an alien monster zooming in and out.'

'I know how everything works,' Annac assured her haughtily. 'I've got to be somewhere.'

'Why not visit Anaru?'

'I think she's having some success.' There was a disapproving edge to Annac's tone. 'She keeps telling me to go away. My brain may be old, but it knows things you two'll never guess.'

'Does it know how to pull you out of a straight plunge to the ground when your wings decide they've had enough?'

'I've been over and inside this thing thousands of times,' Annac protested.

'It must have had a lot wrong with it then.'

'From where I am now, I would say that you are losing your sense of humour,' Annac observed unkindly.

'I am also losing my sanity!' Opu responded so loudly, some of the gathering sunbathers half a mile below them must have heard. 'Let's get out of here before the sun comes up.'

As the pink sun set, Opu guided the unsteady Annac to the ground. 'What do you mean, Anaru's having some success?'

'How should I know? She won't let me in to find out.'

'She hasn't managed to contact anyone in the vicinity of the Kybion, has she?'

'I suppose that's what it's all about. That was what she was trying to do, wasn't it.' Annac was suspicious. 'Why? Why shouldn't she be able to make contact?' Opu remained silent. Annac suddenly understood. 'You haven't heard anything from the Kybion, have you?'

'Taigal Rax still can't contact the android,' Opu whispered as they touched down. 'Don't raise your voice and let everyone else know.' She hustled the retired technician into the station.

'The thing could be malfunctioning.' Though Opu tried to keep her voice down it echoed about the large lobby below the control room. 'Or it just hasn't been able to trace the Star Dancer - or it has, and hasn't been able to do anything about it.'

'Why couldn't it do anything about it? It was given power units capable of blotting out a white dwarf at close range. It should easily have neutralised the thing by now.'

'Assuming the Star Dancer consists of elements we're familiar with. We may think we're pretty clever, but we've never travelled from our planet or interacted with other life forms apart from those who come here.'

'Taigal Rax knows this world though. Why haven't
they come up with any suggestions?'

'They're still trying to fathom out why the Kybion
hasn't contacted them,' Opu admitted. 'This is not
something one of their simple, submerged service
robots on Perimeter 84926 can deal with. They would
have to use the Kybini System to transmit something
more sophisticated, and that would break the legal
level of time interference. The only thing their service
robots are good for is to dismantle the wretched
android - assuming they ever manage to catch it. For
all we know, it could be doing its best to attract the
attention of a Watcher.'

Annac stopped dead as she walked up the ramp
with Opu to the higher levels. 'That means they'll end
up in the same neutron stew as us.'

As the benign, but far from nourishing, pink sun
set, Opu watched the vibrant rays of its yellow energy-
giving companion probe their way above the horizon
for another turbulent shift. She sensed danger in the
air.

Time trickled past and things became so nerve-
shatteringly quiet Opu kept sending out directives to
the other stations to keep them occupied and alert.

When the thunderbolt struck, she was almost
relieved.

The Star Dancer had come in many guises; this
was the most violent yet. It crashed through the
refractor and energy pool of a major station like a
battering ram. The shocked staff fled to the shelter
beneath it. Opu held in the fail-safe for as long as she
dared, while the demolished station was isolated from
the grid. This was the last straw. From now on, the
loss of power could not be compensated for and the
whole system would begin to wind down.

Annac heard Opu observe in a low voice, 'It's
turned really nasty on us this time. It's never behaved

like that before, even when it broke through the shields of Station 73.'

'Wonder what could have upset it?'

'If we don't find out soon, we'll learn what our ancestors felt like when there was a slow eclipse.'

'Unpleasant,' mused Annac. 'It's been estimated their survival chances were only fifty percent. Luckily they didn't have them very often.'

The rest of the shift passed without incident, but the damage had been done. With seven stations completely gone, and the rest with only half-full energy pools, the Ojalie had only a matter of suns before the reserves were depleted. Even if the Star Dancer's attacks stopped, the lost power couldn't be replaced in time.

If the situation hadn't been so desperate, Opu might have ignored the message from Anaru, which simply said, 'contact made'. Although there was only a remote chance the seer and her primitive equipment could help, Opu stealthily left the control after the yellow shift. She was careful not to let Annac suspect where she had gone.

The seer's large circular room was now cluttered with even more apparatus, and Anaru was sitting motionless on the floor on the other side of the light beam curtain. Several shafts of light were playing about her head. Anaru saw Opu. She slapped the flat control disc and shut them down.

'Come in.' There was a marked lack of her innate ebullience. 'I'm not sure whether you're going to like this or not.'

Her manner was off-putting; Opu had been hoping for a more enthusiastic reception, if not good news. 'What's wrong?'

'I've managed to contact a human on Perimeter 84926.'

'And?'

'And I'm not too sure about it at all.'

'Why not?' Opu sat down next to her.

'I can't understand it myself,' Anaru explained. 'I've never seen a creature like it before. Healphani joined the loop to observe. She says it's a human female.'

'And?'

'She reckons we've got a bad one.'

'Why?'

'There's something about the contact that doesn't seem right. Although Healphani can't tell exactly, it seems this human understood what we were telling it a bit too quickly. And it looks somehow wrong to her.'

'You managed to pick it up by following the Kybion's trace?'

'That's the problem. If the human's somehow contacted the Kybion, it might account for her familiarity with the situation. She also managed to rig up some primitive apparatus to boost her telepathic transmitting power.'

'I don't like the sound of that either. This must have something to do with why the Kybion hasn't contacted Taigal Rax. If these humans are as untrustworthy as we've been told, it'll be disastrous if they've managed to interfere with the android.'

'That's not possible, surely?'

Until then, Opu didn't believe the situation could get any worse. 'I wouldn't have thought so before now. I'm beginning to have doubts about a lot of things at the moment. Can I talk to this human?'

'Yes.'

Anaru dashed off to her alcove for a few seconds to raise Healphani and ask her to listen in without the human knowing. She then returned to switch on the multi beam power fields that played about their heads.

'Think simple thoughts,' Anaru warned Opu. 'Their brain capacity is only a fraction of ours.'

'Just more cunning perhaps,' Opu said to herself as an indistinct human image flickered onto the screen.

'Thank you for waiting,' she could hear Anaru think, 'I have the person of importance you wanted to speak to here.'

Trapped on the thought loop, Opu was unable to comment on Anaru's little deception.

'What is your name, human?'

'Tas... Tas...' The apparatus spluttered as it struggled to make the image clear. 'Tasmin is my spirit name.'

'Why do you want to contact me, Tasmin?'

'It is you who want to contact me.'

Opu thought it best not to reply until she knew what this self-assured human looked like. As the image sharpened, the Ojalie were able to see the small skull of a creature wearing something very elaborate piled on top of its head. It possessed no wings. The face had white eyes with coloured dots in the middle of them, a fleshy nose jutted from its centre, and a wide red split beneath that. And it was a very odd colour, though that could have been due to the primitive apparatus the image was being transmitted through.

'Why do I want to speak to you, Tasmin?' Opu asked. 'I doubt that you even know my name.'

'Your name does not matter. If you are the most important person on your planet at the moment, you will want to speak to me. I know what you are looking for, and where it can be found.'

'Then you know where the Kybion is?'

'The Kybion?' The red gash beneath the human's nose moved up at the corners. 'I do not know or care where that deficient machine is.'

Opu's mind worked feverishly to shield her thoughts. Tasmin clearly knew about the android and considered it to be harmless. Could this get even worse?

Opu thought so quickly, the screen flickered furiously.

'Don't do that,' Anaru warned. 'Concentrate.'

Opu pulled her tumultuous thoughts together. 'What is it we are looking for, then?' she demanded.

'A source of such immense energy that it can travel the Galaxy and destroy life on your planet.' The human's thoughts felt cold and matter-of-fact.

'You make it sound as though it had a will of its own?'

'If I knew where it is, we might be able to control it.'

'That I find difficult to believe.'

'Over a century ago the Kybion fitted a young man with the transmitter you designed to attract it. It gave him and three more people longevity. One of those people recently kidnapped the young man. Before Mr Humbert could cut the transmitter from his body, the Star Dancer you are looking for sent his house up in flames. It didn't do Mr Humbert much good at all, I understand. He was such a greedy slug, he probably deserved it. Now the other two of us have a much better idea.'

'Oh yes?' Opu didn't need Healphani to tell her what was coming next.

'If you were to give us the power to control it on this planet, you wouldn't have to worry any more.'

'We'll think about it.' Opu replied, and quickly broke out of the loop before she thought something that would make the human's brain explode.

Anaru had to complete the conversation. 'Now don't go too far away will you, Tasmin?'

Opu was waving her hand, telling her to get rid of the human.

Tasmin faded from the screen and Anaru closed down her power beam to speak to Healphani.

Opu rejoined the loop.

'Well?' she asked before Healphani was able to come into focus. 'What did you make of that?'

'We believe that this human female is indulging in a practice widely used on her planet,' Healphani explained. 'It is called blackmail.'

'Go on.'

'We suspect that were you to supply her with the power she is asking for, she would not use it for the purpose she indicated.'

'Strangely enough I got the same impression. Assuming we had that knowledge and power, we would have to transmit it through Taigal Rax. I assume your regulators wouldn't agree to help us?'

'I'm sure they wouldn't.'

'Thanks.' While Anaru shut down the equipment, Opu sat silently thinking over conversation. Although it wasn't much help, she at least understood a little more of what had been happening. The Kybion had involved four humans for some reason. One carrying the transmitter, one apparently dead, and the remaining two trying to blackmail enough power from her to hold their own world to ransom. Where was the android though? And why didn't Tasmin seem to know what the Star Dancer was? It must have been some sort of manifestation. Or perhaps it was alien to Perimeter 84926 and just decided to make its home there?

Opu became aware that Anaru was scolding her. 'If you don't learn to stop thinking so quickly, you could damage the equipment.'

'It's a pity I can't damage the brain on the other end of it.'

'Well, you can't. There are safety gates in the power field to protect smaller intellects.' Anaru added as an afterthought, 'And they cannot be removed.'

'Well, at least we now know that the Kybion has probably been put out of action,' Opu admitted grudgingly.

'Don't be too despondent.' Anaru seemed to return to her natural self. 'If we've managed to get through to this human, there might be a chance of contacting another.'

'What other? Another one as devious as that? Or one that doesn't know anything about the Kybion or Star Dancer?'

'I have a feeling...' Anaru's orange eyes lit up like flares, 'I have a feeling we are closer than you think.'

'Is it possible to get any closer?'

'If we let this human think she has convinced us, we can insist on contacting the human who has the transmitter.'

Opu hesitated for a second, then realised it was a good idea.

'If we could communicate with the human who has the transmitter,' Opu calculated, 'then we might be able to isolate the energy source. And if the Star Dancer is a sentient entity, we could attempt to make a mind link with it. The only problem is...'

'What?'

'Who is going to be the one to get in the loop with it, and have their brains blasted out through the back of their skull?'

Anaru obviously hadn't thought of that. Her impression of the Universe was a benign one.

'Still,' continued Opu, 'it looks like the only chance we have.'

'What do you want me to do?' Anaru asked apprehensively.

'I'll give you the co-ordinates of the transmitter's signal. It won't interfere with its function if you send the data to Tasmin and let her transmit it. This should bring the human with the transmitter to her and give her some proof of our trust. Make it clear that if she harms the male human it will enrage the Star Dancer.

She'll probably be scared enough to believe it after what happened to their Mr Humbert.'

'It is very deceitful.'

'So what? We're obviously not dealing with straightforward beings.' Opu then insisted, 'Don't tell Annac what we're up to, will you?'

'I wouldn't dare,' Anaru agreed. 'I'll let you know through your control console as soon as something happens.'

CHAPTER 10

A day and night passed in the terraced cottage without Gabrielle and Wendle hardly exchanging a word since their argument. Wendle spent most of the time dozing or writing letters. Gabrielle read about 18th century politics. The only thing to break the monotony was an odd recollection from of one of her dreams, a soft mocking voice. She had no idea who it belonged to. It was explaining some symbols: 'This is the shape that makes atoms fly apart, this the one that can stop time. Another to slow down a rotating pulsar...' Astronomy was not Gabrielle's subject, however, especially when it was that fanciful. Manipulating the structure of the Cosmos couldn't have been on many curriculums, even on the other side of the Galaxy. She returned to the machinations of Georgian government and put the ghostly lesson to the back of her mind.

Eventually the strain of the silence, punctuated only by the gulls and an insistently chirping sparrow, broke Gabrielle's concentration. She made some tea and pushed a mug under the dozing Wendle's nose. 'I'm fed up. I feel like going for a walk. Want to come?'

Wendle looked up at her through half-closed eyes as though examining her motives. Deciding they were genuine, he agreed. 'I know a quiet walk across country where we won't bump into anyone.'

'Far?'

'Far enough,' he answered non-committally. His bruised face still made it uncomfortable for him to talk.

'We'd better leave a message for Weatherby and let him know where we are. He's bound to turn up while we aren't here.'

'Hang Weatherby.'

That solution sounded a bit drastic to Gabrielle, though whatever drove the bouncy policeman's brittle humour, it probably wasn't curable.

While Wendle went to the railway post box to send the letters he'd written the previous night, she jotted down a short note explaining that they had gone for a walk and tucked it under the door knocker.

Wendle was unable to move very fast and needed an umbrella for support. Gabrielle hoped they weren't going too far off the beaten track. Her despised mobile was still at the bottom of her suitcase and she was sure Wendle didn't have one. If he collapsed, she would have to leave him to find help.

After walking side by side in silence for some while, Gabrielle asked hopefully, 'Feeling better?'

'Yes,' murmured Wendle, hardly opening his mouth. 'You?'

'Yes.' He was really asking if Gabrielle was still angry with him. 'Why did you want me to get as far away from here as possible?'

Wendle gave a short sigh. 'It is probably too late now anyway.'

'But this Star Dancer hasn't appeared since the other night. It might have been the fact you were in danger that sparked it off.'

'Probably.'

'So if it looks after you like that, why should I worry about it?'

For the first time since she'd known him, Wendle smiled. It may have been a tight wry smile, but it transformed his face. Gabrielle found his expression both intriguing and chilling, as though he was aware of some cosmic crime. The impression faded when Wendle spoke.

'I did not want you come to any harm. You have got a long while to live yet. And I have lived too long. It would be ridiculous if you were to get killed protecting me.'

'Never thought of it like that. Seems unfair that you were never able to make use of your longevity like the other three - not that I think you'd be dishonest. You should have been allowed a little fun. Were you married when it happened?'

'No, I was never married. I fell in love though. After all this time I can still remember that.'

'Tasmin?'

'Not for very long.'

'What happened?'

'Nemesis sent me a Valentine instead.'

'Wasn't there anyone else before Tasmin?'

'Yes.'

'Didn't she love you enough?'

'Over a century ago, girls married who their fathers allowed them to,' Wendle explained flatly.

'Oh yes, I've heard of something like that nearer home.' Wendle looked at her quizzically. 'Perhaps I was lucky. I'll never know.'

'You would never make a good wife. You have a mind of your own.'

'It's better than depending on someone else's, and I can't have children anyway.'

'Oh?'

'I was seriously injured in a car crash when I was four.'

'You look fit enough now?'

'Apart from the ovaries and smaller pieces of plumbing, they were able to put everything back in the right order. Have to take hormones to stop me from turning into a mountain gorilla...'

Hormones and female plumbing were still a mystery to Wendle. 'I am sure you would never do that.'

'If I start growing a beard, I have to see this consultant. There was one other side effect as well.'

'What was that?'

'Nightmares.' Gabrielle didn't admit that to many people. 'Ever since I can remember, I've been having nightmares.'

'What about?'

'I can never recall them. I only know I've just had one when I wake up sweating or screaming. Even had to have a room to myself in the children's home because of it. That was good, I suppose. Some of the other kids thought I did it on purpose. They never said anything to me about it. Think I scared them for some reason.'

'I wonder why?'

'No idea. I was never a bully, though one little cow did start a rumour that I was a witch.'

'Nightmares are terrible things. I used to have them until I managed to consciously leave my body.'

'Good trick that.' Gabrielle immediately thought of Toby. 'You should teach me.'

'You prefer him to me, don't you?' Wendle suddenly accused.

Gabrielle was fazed for a moment. 'But you are Toby.'

'Not any more. He died of fright that night of the shipwreck.'

'Where is the entrance to this tunnel through the cliff?' Gabrielle asked to divert the uncomfortable conversation.

'Near here. That's how I know this walk.'

'Can I see it?'

Wendle, not keen on the idea, stopped for a moment. 'No, I have not been down there since that night.'

Gabrielle was amazed. 'Why not?'

He didn't reply, just remained stock-still. Some of the colour left the bruises on his face.

'Surely that's the best place to find the Kybion? I thought that was the most important thing now.'

Wendle still hesitated. 'Have you ever been scared? Terrified out of your wits?'

'Well... no,' confessed Gabrielle.

'Fear can make people irrational. Unlike pain, which is difficult to remember because it only makes an impression on the body, terror stamps itself on the mind. If I survived to be a thousand years old, the fear of that night would still be there.' Wendle smiled briefly. 'No - you don't understand, do you? You will never be afraid of anything.'

'Should I be?'

'No. Stay the way you are. Fear is a useless emotion.'

'Show me where the tunnel is.'

Wendle realised that she wouldn't be talked out of it, so went ahead, leading her through a meadow and onto a narrow overgrown path. They walked along an old disused railway track and through a dangerously crumbling tunnel to emerge in a bewildering jumble of brambles and shrubs covering the embankment.

Wendle pointed to halfway up the slope. Gabrielle pushed her way through the bushes to find a slab of rock that had been partially cleared of obstructing weeds.

'Someone's been here quite recently,' she called back to Wendle.

'Are you sure?' he managed to clamber up to her with some difficulty.

'The vegetation covering this rock has been pulled

over it deliberately.'

Gabrielle seized a corner to try and budge it. She pushed it aside far enough to see into a long, dimly lit corridor.

'Don't go down there please,' Wendle implored her. 'It can't be safe.'

'If it isn't, I'll come straight out again,' she reassured him. 'It's lit and looks quite safe.' She eased herself inside. 'I won't be long.'

Wendle stood watching apprehensively through the gap as she jogged down the long corridor into the heart of the cliffs. As it was still lit after all this time it could only mean one thing. His worst fears were about to be confirmed.

Of course, Gabrielle hadn't taken into consideration what she would say to the Kybion if she did meet it. She was too fascinated by her surroundings to be bothered with such tedious eventualities.

The corridor was very long. Fortunately the floor was even and sloped downwards at a slight angle. Eventually she came to several small caves that would have been ideal for smugglers, but there was no contraband and they appeared to be quite empty. Gabrielle went through them to a larger chamber containing bizarre electronic installations. This was high-tech and probably out of bounds. Such a minor eventualities had never bothered her so, at the risk of triggering security sensors, she pressed and pulled a few small prominences in the wall to see what would happen. Each time a cavity behind the rock face was illuminated to show more objects she was unable to identify. Tiring of the game, Gabrielle went on to the next cave. This tied in with the story of where Toby and his companions met the Kybion.

The chamber was filled with water and a wide platform ran along the back of it. Facing it was the exit to the sea.

Gabrielle walked along the platform, examining more wall cavities. When she had reached the far end there was a movement behind her. Not knowing if she was up to meeting a faceless android, she turned very slowly to see what was cutting off her escape. In the dim light she could make out a tall, dark, motionless figure.

Her voice cracked as she called out in creaking tones, 'Who is it?'

'Only me,' sang out a familiar voice. 'I saw your note and followed you.'

'Weatherby! You scared me half to death! Why come all the way down here? It could have waited.'

'Well, Mr Wendle thought you'd been gone a long while. I could tell he didn't want to come down himself, so...' His words trailed off and he looked about at the blinking lights of the electronic equipment. 'Strange sort of place, this. Wonder if all this gear was nicked from somewhere?'

'Yeah, somewhere like NASA. Forget it, policeman. Whoever installed it knew what they were doing and didn't want oiks like us fiddling about with it.'

Weatherby reached out and pressed a sequence of buttons. Bizarre shapes immediately skittered about the water and lit up the chamber like an ice show.

'Idiot!' stormed Gabrielle. 'It wouldn't surprise me if you started that fire at the Grange.'

'It's just this knack I have.'

The shapes faded. Gabrielle held her breath until she was sure nothing else was going to happen. 'I really wish you'd stayed with Toby - Mr Wendle.'

'How did you find this place?'

'We were just walking,' Gabrielle evaded. 'Couldn't this have waited till we got back?'

'Well, I've got this inquisitive nature you see, and...'

'And you thought that, as you didn't trust either of us, you would just follow and see where we went?' She was so annoyed it hadn't occurred to her to ask how he knew where they were. There was nothing in her note because she had no idea where they were going.

'Something like that,' Weatherby admitted as Gabrielle sailed past him, back to the tunnel. 'You've got to admit that you and your frosty friend are a pretty suspicious pair. How am I supposed to know what you were up to the other night?' he called after her.

'You're the detective. You work it out.' Her determined stride made him break into a trot to catch up with her.

'You're still sore at me for making you jump the other night.'

'No, it's the fact you seem to make a habit of it.'

'What is this place anyway?' he asked in an offhand way.

She wasn't fooled that easily. 'You tell me. Is Mr Wendle still waiting out there?'

'I hope so. He could still be in trouble after what I've found out.'

'What have you found out?' Gabrielle demanded.

'I can't tell you. Under that gleaming armour, you're probably a nice sort of girl, and I wouldn't want to see anything happen to you.'

'Why should it?'

'Because you don't have any sense of danger. You behave as though you could walk on water.'

'You nearly scared me to death on two occasions,' she accused.

'That's different. I've got certificates from arch villains to prove I'm harmless. It's just unnatural for anyone not to have a sense of danger.'

'Perhaps I'm just as impervious as my gleaming armour.'

On the long way back, Gabrielle broke into a run. For some inexplicable reason she knew she had to hurry.

She squeezed back through the entrance and leapt down the embankment.

There was no sign of Wendle.

She stood still, looking about, until Weatherby called for her to come and help him through the narrow gap.

'How on earth did you manage to get in there?' she asked absently, though she didn't really care. 'Sure you don't want to tell me what's going on now?' she demanded when he was safely out.

'Eh?' said Weatherby.

'He's gone.'

'Oh hell.'

'It hardly surprises me. He was telling me to get as far away from here as I could only yesterday.'

'That so?' Weatherby seemed interested. 'I wonder why he would tell you that? I can't see any reason unless he's fond of you and getting over-protective.'

Gabrielle laughed. 'I doubt it. If he is, he certainly kept it secret.'

Weatherby seemed reluctant to move while she was still there.

'It's all right, I won't follow you.' She turned and strode off along the track and out of sight through the old railway tunnel.

CHAPTER 11

Wendle could dimly remember collapsing on someone's doorstep after a ten-mile forced walk. He hadn't wanted to take a step of it. Something far stronger than his willpower had dragged him ruthlessly through rough countryside and narrow lanes until he looked like a tramp coming off a route march. Not only

was his usually immaculate appearance dishevelled,
his hair was matted with perspiration, and head
throbbed as though something had been trying to draw
his brain out with a magnet.

He came round smelling heady incense and
glimpsed a green velvet tablecloth. He was in a
panelled and tassel-bedecked room. Everything about
it was so decadent and overwhelming he passed out
again.

The next thing he became aware of was a voice. It
seemed to be a great distance away.

'Hello Toby.'

A woman was standing in front of a window in
direct sunlight. He could only see her shape until she
moved towards him.

'Did you sleep well?' she asked smoothly, her
crinkled hand pushing the tangled hair from his face.

Wendle looked up at the woman, who resembled
an elderly carrot.

'Mrs Angel!' he blurted out.

'Used to be, Toby. Mrs Tavistock now.' She traced a
magenta-nailed finger round his face. 'You've still kept
your looks after all these years, haven't you? Even poor
Tasmin hasn't had that much luck.'

Wendle realised that his limbs wouldn't obey him.
'Why can't I move?'

'Don't worry about that, Toby. No one is going to
hurt you. Not like that horrible Mr Humbert. He told
us all about what he intended to do to you. Going up in
smoke served him right.'

'How did you find out?'

She laughed ominously. 'That nice Mr Weatherby
paid us a visit the other day. Spent quite a lot of time
with us, he did.'

'Aren't you worried he might be back?'

'Goodness no. He'll certainly be back, but won't
bother us. He's only interested in insurance frauds and

sunken ships. Don't worry so much, everything is going to be all right.' Mrs Tavistock's discoloured face wrinkled into a frighteningly insincere smile that told Wendle that nothing could have been further from the truth.

'What are you going to do with me?' he feebly demanded.

'Nothing. We have been told to take special care of you. And as long as you help us, that's just what we'll do.'

Wendle didn't bother to answer. He closed his eyes and pretended to doze off. Eventually there was the rustling of antique taffeta as she left and he sighed with relief. From then on, Wendle knew he had to stay awake for fear of Toby getting the better of his conscious judgement and warning Gabrielle where he was. If he was going to be rescued this time, it would have to be by Weatherby.

***

By the next morning, Gabrielle assumed that Toby had no intention of contacting her. She was angry, though it wasn't surprising after the way Wendle had warned her to keep out of trouble.

She had dreamed again, though. This time she could remember most of it. Some mysterious manifestation was trying to attract her attention. She could even recall its name - Vian Solran. The entity told Gabrielle that it used to eat stars. She laughed, and the ghostly visitor laughed with her. A deity able to destroy suns had swapped the power for a sense of humour. Vian Solran was the entity who had shown her those symbols.

Again she found herself immersed in the same lesson: 'This is the one that can blow comet tails into life, this the one to gather up dangerous asteroids, and this...' While she listened, Gabrielle plucked a symbol

83

from the cloud of codes swimming before her. 'No, no,' said the deity. 'This is for you.' The one Gabrielle held changed into something far less spectacular. 'Keep it until you need it.'

'Need it?'

'Oh yes. You will need it.'

Clutching her dream symbol, Gabrielle woke to discover she was holding her notepad. Disappointed that Toby hadn't given her any message to write on it, she could do nothing but idle the hours away in the hope Weatherby might contact her.

By midday she was even more restless, and so annoyed that she resolved to get on the first train and visit any place on the map that took her fancy. Perhaps it was best to let them get on with things in their own way.

Gabrielle tidied herself up, locked the cottage, and made her way to the station, reading Penny's map. One of the villages on the local line lay next to a lake. This seemed like a cool quiet spot to spend the rest of the day, so she bought a return ticket and sat basking in the sun, waiting for the slow train to arrive at Smuggler's Halt.

***

Wendle resisted the urge to put up a fight when a man and a woman dressed as nurses came to give him another of the injections that kept his mind awake and his body asleep. He thought it would be wiser to save his energy for when Weatherby turned up - if Weatherby turned up.

After a few minutes, to his surprise, he found he was able to get up and walk from the room with the aid of the two attendants. He was led along a corridor lined with gilt-framed mirrors and down several steps into a lower room.

Inside, the air smelt of freesias. He felt strangely

at ease as he was placed in a comfortable armchair facing a transparent box full of copper coils on a circular table. Mrs Tavistock sat one side of it, and facing her was...

'Tasmin!' Wendle blurted out drunkenly. 'How..?'

'A girl has to make a living, my precious,' she smiled.

'But - like this?'

Wendle could read the disdain on Tasmin's heavily painted face. He wished the drugs didn't make him sound such a fool.

She laughed. 'You're still a dreamer aren't you?'

'You've changed.'

'As you're in no condition to say anything intelligent, Toby,' warned Mrs Tavistock, 'be quiet.'

One of the nurses placed what felt like earphones over Wendle's head. 'What's this?'

'We would like you to talk to someone, Toby,' Tasmin's voice explained over the headgear even though her lips didn't move. 'Don't be alarmed. We promise it won't hurt you at all. We have discovered some friends many millions of miles away from here.' She spoke as though he was a six-year-old rather than a man who had lived for a hundred and twenty-seven years. 'We can't see them, I'm afraid, but they have proved that we can trust them. They want to help you out of the dreadful situation that terrible machine put you in.'

'This equipment will help you concentrate,' Mrs Tavistock explained. 'You will hear someone ask you questions. You only need think your replies. Don't try to fight the machine. It is very powerful and could fry your brain if you do not do exactly as you are told. Do you understand?'

'Why?' murmured Wendle.

'I'm not explaining it all again,' Tasmin snapped aloud.

'Why what, Toby?' asked Mrs Tavistock.

'Changed... she's changed.'

'Don't be foolish. No one has remained in love with the same person for over a century.' She waved to a nurse. 'He's becoming distraught. Give him another injection.'

Cold, numbing desolation returned and Wendle's ability to make sense of his own words fled.

He watched, speechless, as Tasmin pressed a switch attached to the side of the table and pulled down a lever on the case of coiled copper. A band of energy rose into the air, encircling the table and the three people sitting at.

'Ready?' Mrs Tavistock asked Tasmin.

'Ready.' Tasmin adjusted the headset through her elaborate hairdo.

A coil of white light appeared in the centre of the table. It was spinning like a top, and then gradually steadied itself until it was upright and humming evenly.

'Hello, hello,' Wendle could hear Tasmin call. 'Anaru, are you there?'

'I am,' said another, fainter voice.

Wendle realised that the two women hadn't been joking about talking to someone millions of miles away - they had to say something because light years, like other vagaries of the modern world, were beyond their stoically Victoria comprehension.

'I have brought the man with the transmitter here as your Controller Opu instructed?'

'Opu has had an accident.'

Wendle could feel Tasmin immediately tense.

'She was caught in an explosion. I am afraid you will have to deal with me until she has been replaced,' Anaru explained.

'But I understood your situation is critical? You told me that you didn't have much time left?'

'Controller Opu was installing a valve to make the remaining energy inaccessible to the Star Dancer when the explosion occurred. She was successful, but it must eventually be opened, otherwise Ojal will starve. It has merely bought us a little time.'

'I see,' Tasmin mused calculatingly. 'So you still need to trace the Star Dancer?'

'Of course,' Anaru insisted. 'But we cannot negotiate anything with you until we have another controller-in-charge. I'm sure you understand that?'

'Oh yes,' Tasmin was obviously relieved that they were still in dire danger. 'When will this be?'

'There is much for her to do when selected, though I think it likely you will be given priority. Whatever you do, please keep in the contact zone, and do not move the transmitter.'

'All right. Do you want to talk to the young man?'

'Yes.'

'His name is Toby,'

Tasmin reached across to flick a switch on the equipment.

'Toby,' said an alien voice inside his head. 'Can you hear me?'

Wendle froze as Anaru kept repeating the name 'Toby' and he felt as though his soul was being prised from his body.

Then his mind heard the voice of a young man protesting, 'I can hear you... Stop calling me... I cannot move.'

'What is the matter, Toby?' the alien voice went on. 'You must not fight the loop.'

'You must not call me Toby. Toby is not Wendle... He cannot come...'

Mrs Tavistock realised that something was dreadfully wrong. 'Shut the power down!' she snapped.

Wendle's eyes were suddenly motionless, and his body slumped back in the armchair.

'You've killed him you silly little fool!'

Tasmin instantly shut down the equipment and gazed at the lifeless body of her Victorian lover. 'Oh hell! What do we tell them now?'

***

'Interesting,' mused Opu. She had been listening to the conversation outside the loop.

'Probably put too much power through him,' Anaru deduced. 'Seems as though he's dead by the way they behaved. If that's the case, you won't be raising any Star Dancer.'

She was about to shut off the power when Opu called out, 'No! Don't! Leave it on.'

'I can't keep the frequency idle for long. It can interfere with other planets using the same signal.'

'Don't you understand?'

Anaru gave her a blank look.

'He kept insisting his name wasn't Toby. He may have originally been the Toby who should have died one of their centuries ago, then that interfering machine gave him longevity.'

'So?'

'So it's possible his mind wasn't able to stand the strain of existence, unlike the other three, and it gradually began to reject his body. Although it went on living, his spirit refused to accept the idea and tried to claim back his personality. Toby perhaps rejected immortality years before, yet was tied to it in the absence of death.'

Slowly Anaru's face lit up. 'Because I kept calling his name, it was enough to make his spirit break free of his body. So, although Wendle's dead, Toby's spirit could still be around and not know how to return to the evolutionary spiral.'

'It may be here with us, or waiting on Perimeter 84926 for us to call it again. If we can make contact, it may be able to tell us what this Star Dancer is.'

Anaru didn't waste time replying. She disconnected the link to Healphani, who had been listening in, and increased the power to the chamber where Tasmin and Mrs Tavistock were still sitting.

The two women had to dive beneath the table to escape the scouring surge of energy that swept the room in an explosion of light.

In an instant it was gone, and so was Wendle's body.

CHAPTER 12

Gabrielle stepped from the train. On the other side of the station's white picket fence the footbridge led down to a neat terrace of flint faced houses, and a gently sloping path ran towards the inviting lake she had seen on the map. Gabrielle wended her way down the uneven pavement. Overlooking the lake was a large Victorian house with a monkey puzzle tree and high gates. The rest of the village appeared friendly enough and it was anachronistic to find a house so well fortified. Perhaps an eccentric billionaire lived there. Gabrielle had encountered all the wealthy tyrants she wanted to for one lifetime and crossed the road to reach the cool expanse of water. The lake lay calm and dark green, spangled with a profusion of pastel water lilies. The only movement in the water was caused by the flow from a weir beneath a bridge on the far side.

Gabrielle stood under the branches of a willow for a moment. It was cool under the lacy curtain of leaves, and she turned lazily to see who was making the rapid footsteps so out of place in the quiet village. It was certainly no tourist. He was dressed in a navy blue suit and trench coat, and his bouncy gait was instantly recognisable. She retreated further into the willow's concealing curtain and wondered what coincidence could have brought Weatherby to the same unlikely place.

Gabrielle was tempted to dash out and surprise him in the same way that he had nearly frightened the life out of her, but curiosity held her back. If Weatherby was here, then it was more than likely Wendle was as well.

The policeman went to the large fortified house. After nosing about the front for a few minutes, he disappeared round the back of the place.

Gabrielle sank to the carpet of soft grass beneath the willow, and smiled wryly to herself. As the surprise wore off, questions started to crowd her mind. What if it hadn't been a coincidence? Toby had led her to Wendle on other occasions; now something else seemed to be doing the same thing.

The thought took her aback.

What if the transmitter was attracting her? How could she have anything in common with the mysterious Star Dancer that had arrived and departed so conveniently, so destructively? True, it had rescued Wendle, Weatherby and herself from a very unpleasant death, and something had weakened gratings and unbolted doors so she could find Wendle. It seemed as though the Star Dancer had been following her about. A thought so dreadful crossed her mind, and her blood ran cold as she let out an audible gasp of horror.

Gabrielle quickly glanced about as though finding herself in another dimension. All she could see were the willow branches. With difficulty, she made herself to relax as she had been taught in hospital as a child, and cleared her mind of all thoughts. There was no breeze and the long strips of leaves hung motionless before her. Very lightly, as though gathered up by invisible threads, the curtains of willow were drawn gently aside. She rose and walked through them. They fell back into position again.

Gabrielle had an answer of a kind. An answer more difficult to believe than the story Wendle had told her about meeting a machine from another world, though it would explain why she could never remember her nightmares, and why Wendle wanted her to go away before the Kybion found her. And what would happen if the android hunting the Star Dancer did catch her? Gabrielle shuddered. If she really had this sort of power, it was unlikely even an alien machine would be able to do anything about it.

Gabrielle walked alongside the lake, pondering. Just to make sure this wasn't a waking nightmare, she lifted the occasional water lily from the lake with her mental energy, and then let it drop back down again. As she did so, the birds stopped singing, and something grey and small fled so rapidly at her approach it wasn't possible to tell if it was a cat or squirrel.

Of course Gabrielle had been drawn to Wendle. She was the Star Dancer.

It was too incredible for her human mind to take in all at once. With the energy stolen in her spirit form from another planet, her power far exceeded the intellectual capacity to control it. But she would have to try. Gabrielle couldn't bear to think that she was about to annihilate an alien species, or the fact that Toby had been living in his cage of longevity for so long, just waiting for her to turn up.

The teenager's mind continued to balk at the horrific revelation and she found herself pacing her own respiration as though fearful of breathing out flames. With half a dozen airline tickets she could stop as many wars - or more likely start them. What if she sneezed and the airliner blew up? Could she fly away, or save the other passengers? Given the power craved by the human race ever since it discovered it had a thumb that opposed its fingers, Gabrielle hadn't the faintest idea what to do with hers. She had to give the stolen energy back. In heart and mind she was no Shiva. Some would have revelled in the ability to destroy worlds. She found the awareness bleak and depressing. Apart from that... she had never been so confused in her life.

Gabrielle compelled herself to do a complete circuit of the lake before making any decision. The consequences of making the wrong one didn't bear thinking about.

She was once again standing by the willow tree when the intangible something that had been attracting her to the place was suddenly no longer there. Perhaps the transmitter had malfunctioned or Wendle had been killed? But no, she could detect it transmitting again. From where, she had no idea.

Gabrielle was unable to delay any longer. She must learn to leave her body as Toby had done.

In the shade of the willow she once again cleared her mind and concentrated on Toby. There was a faint shape moving with the sunbeams that danced through the lattice of leaves. Unable to bring it into focus, Gabrielle closed her eyes and saw Toby in his Victorian costume, more distinct than he had ever been before. He raised his thin hands, almost concealed by the frilled cuffs of his cream shirt, and beckoned her to follow him. It was difficult at first, but the more Gabrielle relaxed, the freer her consciousness became from her body. She rose to join him and looked back at herself, sitting beneath the willow tree. She had done it.

Toby started to grow fainter as though he was being eased from one spiritual plane into another. It was now obvious that Wendle had died and Toby was no longer bound to his mortal body.

Gabrielle felt a sense of relief. At long last he had

been released from the existence he so hated. Now she had to rectify the damage her marauding spirit had been doing and follow the signal of Wendle's transmitter. It was far away and it was up to her monstrous subconscious to lead her conscious thoughts to the planet.

The journey started gently enough, albeit at the speed of thought. But thoughts are difficult to control. Hesitating to wonder at Saturn and its myriad rings, they were suddenly catapulted into deep space. Gabrielle wondered if she was still in the same Universe. The signal remained steady so she tried to take a tighter grip on the reins and not let her subconscious bolt again.

Gabrielle went past worlds and suns on a path that she now recognised. Much to her frustration, her attention hovered and weaved through cosmic spectacles at a leisurely rate and there was nothing she could do to hurry it on. One instant she was flapping like a butterfly through a porridge of semi-solid gases, the next soaring into the solar wind of a crimson sun in a ball of glowing white fire. If this was what she was doing while she slept, it was hardly surprising she had nightmares.

One place Gabrielle's subconscious seemed especially intrigued with was a huge transparent construction the size of a planet and fashioned like a gyroscope. It spun slowly in its own orbit about a sun. Given the massive engines that powered it, the structure must have been capable of leaving one solar system to visit others. She meandered about its spacious, sparkling decks made of solid diamond. Through the glittering walls she could see the imaginative creatures who had built it all, living in their own self-contained ecosystems. These engineers were constructing something huge in the centre of the gyroscope. When it was finished, the main body of the world would be opened to release it.

All this dawdling wasn't going to help Gabrielle find her destination. She tried to jar more urgency into her subconscious. It was no good. It paid no attention her body's concept of time. Now her thoughts had been freed, they knew that if they rushed, she would arrive at exactly the same time as if she had let her subconscious make the journey in its own way. Even though Gabrielle now understood this, she was still afraid of not arriving in time to save a whole species from dwindling out of existence.

The transmitter's signal became stronger.

Suddenly Gabrielle found herself surrounded by orange eyed creatures flying to find space on high ground before their pink sun set. They didn't notice her descend to a hotchpotch of round buildings, somehow managing to cling to each other like a colony of honey fungus. A signal from one of the lower rooms summoned her to enter through a curtain of coloured light beams. Gabrielle was aware of becoming visible.

It was then she understood the history of this strange world: its formation, its suns, its ancient beliefs, and modern hedonism. In every Ojalie's mind there was a name for her - Star Dancer. They believed her to be the deity born from Vian Solran, a primeval quasar... devourer of stars, disrupter of the Galaxy, and any other cosmic disaster they could blame her for. Gabrielle was desperate to correct their misconception and in the room behind the light beam curtain sat the only Ojalie she could communicate with.

Another figure with a large skull and wings open in horror was also inside the seer's loop. The Ojalies' glowing orange eyes were gazing intently at something lying before them in the centre of the loop.

Gabrielle moved into the invigorating energy flowing round them and looked down. On the floor, in a pile of dust, lay a small blinking sphere. It seemed to be winking at her.

She was looking at the transmitter Wendle had been carrying inside him for so many years.

CHAPTER 13

Anaru's spontaneous experiment had scoured the room where Tasmin, Mrs Tavistock, and Wendle sat. Instead of dragging Toby's spirit to join them in the loop, Wendle's crumpled body suddenly appeared.

Opu could feel herself panicking. 'You used too much power!'

Anaru caught her breath and watched Wendle's body rapidly disintegrate. 'It's just as well he was already dead.'

'Our atmosphere would have killed him instantly anyway. We'd better make sure Annac never finds out about this. She'll think we've been using the Kybini System on living tissue. That would make her really angry, especially as she never managed to work out how to do it herself.'

'That's the least of our worries.'

'What now?' Opu hadn't anticipated anything worse than impending annihilation.

'Apparently something the human had was a little more resilient. Look.' Anaru pointed to the pile of dust, all that remained of Wendle. In it sat the small blinking sphere he had been carrying for over a century.

'Now we have the transmitter,' Opu was too petrified to raise her voice. 'That was not quite what I had in mind.'

'Could we use the Kybini System to transport it somewhere else before the Star Dancer turns up?'

'There won't be time, and we have to make contact with the entity anyway.'

'Telepathic contact is one thing; I'm not too keen

on sitting in the same room with the energy of a small
sun. I've been hardened to most things over the years,
but sudden incineration has not been one of them.'

'You'd better go and tell control what's happened.'

'I can't do that,' Anaru protested. 'You're not a seer
and could never handle this equipment.'

'What's the chance of us communicating with the
Star Dancer?'

'At close range? We'll have to leave the loop.'

Reluctantly Opu obeyed. 'How long?'

'Impossible to say. Entities like this don't have the
same sense of time as us. It could already be here.'

'Could it be a spirit?'

'The conscious spirit of living energy? Let's hope it
has an intellect, as opposed to being just cosmically
enraged.'

'You're reassurance incarnate.'

Opu and Anaru stretched their wings and waited.

The dust that had once been Wendle's body began
to gently scatter. Without warning a pillar of energy
was towering before them inside the loop, drinking the
power from Anaru's equipment. It made no sound,
which was more terrifying than if it had roared with
rage.

'It *is* a spirit,' the seer whispered. 'I can sense it.'

'Well, let's hope it's friendly,' Opu muttered into
her beak.

A shape started to form in the blindingly bright
energy.

'It looks like a human.' Anaru gasped.

'They can't be that backward if they can do this.'
Opu looked up at the small-skulled creature perched
on top of ridiculously long legs. She was tempted to
reach out and touch the glowing form.

'Don't do that! There's enough power to incinerate
this side of the city!'

Opu pulled back quickly, wondering how she could

have been so idiotic. The strange long-limbed creature with streaming hair entwined by swirling ribbons of energy was so fascinating, she almost forgot that Ojal's survival was dependent on her wits.

'What do you want here?' Anaru asked as Opu was taking an uncomfortable length of time to collect her senses.

If the creature understood she was trying to contact it, there was no sign.

Opu's presence of mind at last returned. 'Do you know what you're doing to our planet? Are you here in your natural form? Do you understand what we're saying?'

The Star Dancer remained motionless, gazing at a point in infinity.

'Perhaps we can only talk to it through the loop?' Opu was about to re-enter the dome of energy marbled with veins of plasma that was made by the Star Dancer.

'Don't be so idiotic!' shrieked Anaru. 'This is pure energy! It will carbonise you!'

'We have to contact it. It must have intellect of some sort.'

'You cannot go into the loop. Just keep talking to it.'

'It's no use. It's probably only here because the transmitter brought it. It may not even be aware of our existence.' Opu turned back to the Star Dancer. 'If you understand us, try to give a sign.'

'What sign?' asked Anaru.

'Don't interfere.'

Anaru was only too pleased to be let off the hook and kept quiet.

'Can't you wave or something? Stop looking at that wretched transmitter for a second.'

Opu didn't need to be psychic to know what it wanted. She sighed. 'All right then, I'll smash it if that's what you want.'

'Suicidal fool!' squawked Anaru.

'Shut up. We have to make contact before it loses interest in the transmitter. This is the only chance we'll get.' She looked intently at the Star Dancer. 'I am going to reach out and smash the transmitter. If you understand me, go to the nearest refractor station. If you don't leave the loop instantly, I'll be killed.' Opu tensed herself in preparation.

'No, Opu. It's not worth the risk.'

'There's no other way. If it fails, you must contact main control and let them know what's happened.'

'Don't do it!'

Opu's orange eyes glowed with the reflection of the Star Dancer's energy. She took a deep breath, and then plunged her hand into the loop.

When she came to, Opu felt as though the ancient buildings above had fallen on her. Gradually she was aware of her throbbing hand. Anaru had shut the loop down and was pulling a fragment of the transmitter out of her palm.

'It's gone,' Anaru said.

'How long?' asked Opu.

'Seconds ago. As soon as you broke the loop it left.'

'Then it understood! It must be at the station!'

'You can't fly in that condition.'

'I doubt if it'll wait for me to walk there, and you know what the shuttle service is like in the old sector.' Opu staggered to the balcony and flapped her wings to make sure they were still operational.

'Be careful!' she heard Anaru call as she leapt into the sky of the newly rising yellow sun.

Opu flapped as fast as she dared towards the refractor station. The gathering sunbathers below looked up. They wondered whether the strain of everything was too much for the controller-in-charge and she had become suicidal.

The shields of the refractor station were slowly opening. Hanging menacingly above them was the Star Dancer.

Opu dropped onto the control room balcony and staggered into the room. Without explanation, she moved the operator at the main console aside and seized the lever that opened the energy pool to the other stations. As she pushed it home, cries of anguish echoed around the control.

'It'll drink the whole system dry!'

'She's taken leave of her senses!'

'Somebody shut the shields!'

Opu locked the lever in position. 'If anybody shuts the shields, all the energy we've lost from the pools will spill over the city and cremate everyone out there.'

'But..?' whimpered a bewildered voice.

'Watch, will you, just watch.'

The staff apprehensively lined the control room window to look at the huge ball of energy hovering above the open shields.

The Star Dancer had dispensed with its human form. It slowly rotated, growing larger. The staff in the control room began to murmur amongst themselves in terror until it covered the massive pool that the shields had left unguarded.

Then it hung in the sky like a third sun.

All the sunbathers in the vicinity swiftly fled.

The Star Dancer began to pulsate slowly, and then faster and faster, until it was a shimmering sphere larger than the refractor. A coil of energy spiralled down to dip into the energy pool. The control room staff, thinking it was only a matter of seconds before it drank the remainder dry, were unable to understand why the power level didn't move.

Then the needle erratically flickered into life. The level slowly but surely rose. The great ball of energy outside grew smaller and smaller. All the stations that were still operational were being brought back to their normal capacity. By the time the energy-giving transfusion was over, the Star Dancer was just a speck of light twinkling in the yellow sun's rays.

Opu's knees gave way, and she fainted.

***

'Why didn't you tell me what was going on?' Opu could hear Annac's gruff tones call as she landed on the balcony of her home and came in. 'You could've been killed you know.'

'I nearly was on several occasions,' Opu sat up slowly, wondering how long she had been unconscious. 'I feel as though I've been drinking neat sunlight from the energy pool. My inside must be like a condemned zone.'

'Serves you right,' snapped Annac. She was suddenly aware of someone else standing beside her on the balcony. 'Who are you?' she demanded.

'I'm Opu's gene partner,' was the breezy reply. An untidy bundle of something under her arm squawked in agreement.

'Good grief.' Annac looked down at the wriggling creature. 'Is that what you managed between you then?'

Anapa laughed thankfully. 'Well, Opuna's more hers than mine. She's been worrying me to bring her back ever since she left home.'

Opu glowered. 'And you brought her as soon as it was possible of course.'

'Well, everyone kept telling me how cruel it was to keep you two apart once the emergency was over.'

Annac smiled to herself. The prospect of Opu now having to look after her horrible child again more than compensated for having been kept out of her confidence. She turned and fluttered unsurely off to the peace of retirement, futile inventions, and her own home.

CHAPTER 14

The burst of energy that had scoured the room where Mrs Tavistock and Tasmin had been transmitting their messages to Anaru left as suddenly as it had come. The two nurses attending Wendle took fright and fled for their lives.

'Toby's gone!' shrieked Tasmin, more in terror than remorse.

'I can see that, you silly little fool!' Mrs Tavistock shrieked back. They must have tricked us!'

'I knew it was wrong to try and deal with creatures millions of years more advanced than us,' Tasmin whined.

'Don't be such a stupid minx. Toby was dead anyway. Now they have the transmitter, they also no doubt have the creature that has been draining their planet of energy - and I'm sure that's going to do them a lot of good.'

'Oh...' Tasmin sniggered, and then started to giggle. 'That'll make things even worse for them won't it?' An unannounced visitor standing in the doorway interrupted her mirth.

'May I join in the joke, ladies?' Weatherby enquired, as though inviting himself to a tea party.

'What are you doing here?' demanded Mrs Tavistock.

'I took the liberty of coming in as your other two companions were leaving.' He beamed. 'They seemed quite upset by something, so I thought I would just pop in to see if everything was all right.'

'Liar! You were snooping. I knew you would be back.'

'Now why is everyone so suspicious of me?' Weatherby had an air of offended innocence that wouldn't have fooled a four-year-old. He looked over the strange equipment and noticed the singed lace on Mrs Tavistock's cap. 'Something scorch the top of your head, Mrs T? I wonder what could have done that?'

'Why don't you go away? We've told you everything we know about Mr Gunn.'

'But it isn't Mr Gunn I'm interested in this time.'

'Who then?' demanded Tasmin. 'Who else could we know anything about?' She was unable to resist snatching a glance at the armchair where Wendle had been sitting only minutes before.

'Fair-haired fellow, not very tall.' Weatherby added pointedly, 'Age unknown.'

'What do you mean, "age unknown?"' asked Mrs Tavistock frostily.

'Well, ladies, he was rather like you in many ways. For some reason it was very difficult to discover when he was born. And what I did find out seems to suggest he must have been a hundred and twenty-seven years old, about the same age as the "young" lady here. Now there's no law against living for as long as you like, I'm pretty sure, but as Mr Gunn seemed to have the same problem, it brought me round to thinking that you all must have been connected in some way more binding than passing acquaintance.'

Under cover of the table Mrs Tavistock pulled a derringer from her gown. 'Congratulations, Mr Weatherby.'

'Congratulations, Mrs T?' inquired Weatherby.

'Congratulations because you had managed to convince me you were quite a fool. What else do you know?'

'I know that after Mr Gunn had finished with him, Mr Wendle was in a pretty poor state. Though I wouldn't accuse you two ladies of being so heavy-handed, I also know he arrived here yesterday and, in his delicate condition, might easily come to some harm without proper attention.'

Tasmin tried to sound amazed at his suggestion. 'What harm?'

'Now, now, ladies,' sighed Weatherby. 'Where is Mr Wendle? I'm sure we can't keep this conversation up forever.'

Mrs Tavistock suddenly smiled. 'All right Mr Weatherby. Please sit down. We will try to explain.' She indicated the chair Wendle had been sitting in, much to the barely suppressed horror of Tasmin. 'You may pass me the head piece.'

Weatherby strode nonchalantly over and picked the headset out of its seat. He handed it to Mrs Tavistock and sat down.

'Thank you,' said Mrs Tavistock with one of her off-putting creased smiles. 'Now, I am going to tell you something you may find it difficult to believe, so just make sure you listen right through to the end, Tasmin is going to make sure you don't move.' She produced the derringer and pointed it at his head. 'So don't move!' Weatherby gave a disingenuous pout of complaint, yet remained still while Tasmin wound two leads tightly round his wrists, and connected them to the equipment's terminals.

'You are no doubt aware of the current that can run through that flex: you're obviously not the buffoon you have been trying to make out you are, Mr Weatherby, so don't try doing anything that would make Tasmin pull that lever,' Mrs Tavistock warned him.

'This is going to be quite a long story by the sound of it, Mrs T. Are you sure you want to keep pointing that pistol at my head all the way through it?'

'I am going to be as brief as possible.'

'Good, I wouldn't like to keep you ladies from your tea and vitamin pills.'

'Shut up and listen,' Mrs Tavistock said so forcefully that he obeyed. 'Over a century ago, Tasmin,

Mr Humbert, Toby Wendle, and me were escaping
from a ship foundering in the Channel. Our lifeboat
was washed into a cavern concealed in the cliffs. We
were exploring this cavern when a machine appeared
and told us we all had to die, otherwise our survival
would disrupt time. Then it changed its mind and
decided to use Toby Wendle by fitting him with a
transmitter that would-'
     Weatherby interrupted. 'Attract a powerful entity
that had been taking trips to a planet on the other side
of the Galaxy and sucking dry the energy pools the
inhabitants lived on?'
     'How did you know that?' Mrs Tavistock
demanded.
     'Toby Wendle must have told him,' panicked
Tasmin.
     'Shut up girl! Keep your hand on that lever.'
     Weatherby sighed. 'No. No one told me, not even
poor Mr Wendle.'
     'Poor Mr Wendle?'
     'You killed him, didn't you? You thought you would
be clever and try to grab all that power for yourselves,
but forgot that Toby was never tied to this world in the
same greedy, materialistic way you are. He didn't want
to go on living forever like a mouldering vegetable. So
he got out as soon as the opportunity presented itself.'
     'How do you know all that if he didn't tell you?'
shrieked Tasmin.
     'How do you think?' Weatherby asked innocently.
He beamed a smile at them. It was light years away
from his usually amiable one.
     Mrs Tavistock swayed in shock for a second, trying
to take in what he was saying. 'It's impossible. We
removed the markers! You couldn't have traced us so
easily!' She raised the derringer and fired its two shots
at point blank range into Weatherby's chest.
     Weatherby didn't flinch. He looked down and blew

the pulverised remains of the bullets away from his satin waistcoat.

'It's the Kybion,' Tasmin whimpered. In desperation she pulled the lever and circulated enough volts through his body to vaporise Frankenstein's monster.

A halo of energy saturated Weatherby.

It had no effect.

Tasmin kept forcing the lever down harder and harder.

'Switch it off!' Mrs Tavistock screamed.

Tasmin was deafened by the noise of the equipment and too panicked to hear.

The coils inside the transparent case started to spark against each other. Flames seared through the container, melting it. Still Weatherby sat there, impassively watching the two women lose control and scream abuse at each other.

With the flex round his wrists still attached to the terminals, he reached inside his waistcoat.

The two women froze. They gazed disbelievingly at each other across the table. Each could see the other's skin shrinking back to the contours of the skull. The creases and wrinkles became folds in the living flesh. Tasmin's make-up was dragged into grotesque lines about her face, and Mrs Tavistock's features crumpled like a mouldy orange. Then the two women shrank inside their Victoria dresses.

Tasmin held resolutely onto the lever.

The flames from the molten remains of the transparent casing licked greedily at the plaster decoration on the ceiling. The current being generated on the table reached a peak and the equipment exploded into a fireball that engulfed all three of them. The ceiling caved in. The building was soon ablaze.

This time, the fire brigade sent a full attendance in twenty minutes, but twenty minutes is a long time for a greedy fire to be left to its own devices. The local residents turned out in force to see the conflagration. Many left their jobs, either in shops or picking strawberries in the fields.

'Must've been burning those ruddy candles again,' an old man said to the black stranger in a trench coat standing beside him.

'That so?'

'Yes,' the old man went on, convinced of his facts. 'That weird old bird and her friend were always up to something odd. You could see them lights flickering through the windows at night as though it were Christmas.'

'Odd?' joined in a neighbour. 'Those two were odd all right, and I'm not so sure about the other pair who dashed off to the railway station not so long before this happened.'

'What pair?' Weatherby asked her.

'Looked like nurses. The old girl always looked pretty sick to me. Wouldn't be surprised if they didn't have something to do with it. Well, a place with that much security must've had valuables in it.'

'Really?' enquired Weatherby so pointedly that the woman understood.

'Are you a plainclothes policeman?' she asked as though that was the only explanation for the slightly eccentric appearance of the stranger.

Weatherby produced his identification from an embroidered waistcoat pocket. The woman glanced at it, and the old man seized hold of his wrist to pull his hand closer for a better look.

'Struth,' he exclaimed as he touched Weatherby's metal watchstrap. 'You feel as though you're on fire as well.'

'I have a very warm disposition,' Weatherby explained impassively as he replaced his ID. 'Small children and animals think I'm marvellous. It's only adults who don't care for me much.'

'Don't suppose you have to arrest many small children and animals, do you?' The old man laughed, putting the heat of the watchstrap down to his own ageing sense of touch. 'You want us to make some sort of statement then?'

'It seems you could be very helpful in assisting us with our investigations. So if you wouldn't mind..?' At those words, Weatherby turned to see a queue of local residents waiting to offer up statements.

The fire had effectively gutted the building and the firefighters were paddling about in the remains, so it seemed as though he was going to be the next attraction.

CHAPTER 15

As pins and needles shot through her arms, Gabrielle twitched and woke to find herself surrounded by a curtain of willow leaves.

The now familiar smell of smouldering wood met her nostrils. Water from firefighters' hoses was trickling down the bank and into the lake. Before she could part the leaves to see what had happened, there was an amiable voice.

'Feeling all right?'

Gabrielle jerked round to see Weatherby sitting under the tree with her.

'What...?'

He smiled. 'You must have slept well to miss that. Suppose I should be glad you hadn't managed to find your way inside this time.'

'What happened?' She could now see the remains of the Victorian house through the willow. 'That was the place I saw you nosing about earlier,' she accused.

Weatherby lifted his hands in innocence. 'Well, don't blame me. Apparently the ladies had the habit of playing with candles.'

'Wendle's dead, isn't he?'

'I reckon he was inside the building with the other two when it went up. Fire Officer doesn't think he'll find enough for a decent autopsy, but they can even get a DNA match from lipstick nowadays.'

'I doubt he was there to see his girlfriend.'

'Bad metaphor.'

'Where would you find a sample of his DNA to match it with anyway?'

'You'd be surprised.'

Gabrielle said nothing. She was having enough trouble digesting the truth of her own identity. Then something occurred to her. 'You didn't really think I was in there as well, did you?'

'But you weren't. I couldn't stand the thought of a young thing like you going up in flames, or coming to any sort of harm for that matter.'

'You sound as though you really meant that.'

'I do. It was never in me to let anyone get hurt. I don't think like that.'

Gabrielle believed Weatherby. If she didn't have other things on her mind, she would have felt guilty about the names she had called him.

Even though a tremendous weight had been lifted from her mind, her legs were unsteady when she tried to rise and she toppled over.

'Careful,' said Weatherby, catching her. 'You must have been fast asleep. I think I'd better take you back in my car.'

'Haven't you got a lot to do after the fire?' Gabrielle asked, though she was grateful for the offer.

'Sure, but it's unlikely those three will be plotting any more insurance frauds, or anything else for that matter, so there's no hurry.'

After Weatherby had seen her back to the cottage, Gabrielle slept soundly until the next morning.

When she woke, she realised that the nightmares

had gone for good. Her senses were heightened. If she wanted, she could see colours beyond the visible spectrum, tune into music being played on a passing cruise ship, and read the frustration in the calls of herring gulls telling fledged chicks to feed themselves - the message went somewhere along the lines of, "leave home and get a life before I break your wings."

Gabrielle wondered if she dared go out into this brave new world and risk mental overload. But this power wasn't caused by the hormonal surge of adolescence; she was special, and could control the gift. The teenager understood none of it, though accepted the responsibility with her practical outlook, knowing that one life was just a blink in time. If she got it wrong, she could always get back on the wheel at the same place and try again.

It was still early when Gabrielle put on her walking shoes and trudged along the beach to the village to return her library book and buy some groceries. She resisted the temptation to visit Wendle's bungalow on the way, and arrived just as the library was being opened.

She handed the book back and apologised with a smile, 'I found it difficult to get into. Things kept distracting me.' Then she selected a volume twice as thick on the Napoleonic Wars and strode off to the grocer where she met Dot.

'What did he say then?' she asked.

Gabrielle managed to grin. 'Not much.'

'Didn't think he would.'

On the way back, Gabrielle was unable to pass the bungalow and walked down the slope. The door was unlocked. Everything had been tidied up. The mugs they had been drinking from had been picked up from the floor, washed, and placed on the draining board. Wendle couldn't have done it, and it was even more unlikely one of the locals was responsible. Gabrielle

wandered about the living room looking at it with her
new acuity, yet touching nothing. Then, feeling as
though she was trespassing, she wound up the
grandfather clock, and left.

***

In the caverns under the cliffs, Weatherby was fiddling
with the controls on the monitor in the main chamber.
An image flickered into life.

A silver-scaled Taigalian peered accusingly at him
and announced gravely, 'You are one of the most
incompetent androids ever to be designed.'

'Why?' asked Weatherby in less than genuine
amazement.

'Why have you waited until the emergency was
over before contacting us?'

'What was there to tell you? You never
programmed me to contact you every few minutes,
Besides, I was busy.'

The silver figure decided to try another tack. 'Why
didn't you neutralise the energy source as soon as you
discovered it?'

'Well, I couldn't kill the young girl, could I? She
didn't know what she was doing, and when she did
realise she was able to put it right.'

'You did nothing. You are totally useless. You will
dismantle yourself and cease functioning. You cannot
even be trusted to gather elementary data about the
planet.'

'I can walk under water.'

'That was not your prime function,' the Taigalian
snapped.

'And I've got a good job in the police force. They
might even give me a commendation after clearing up
those insurance frauds.'

'You were programmed to take the appearance of a
human being. You have not been instructed to become

one.'

'But I like it. It's comfortable inside this body. Anyway,' Weatherby announced, 'there's nothing you can do about it.' He switched the monitor off and strolled back out of the tunnel, laughing to himself as he went, 'Nothing - Nothing at all.'

***

The first moon had reached its meridian. The silver light bathed the platform onto which shimmering bodies had climbed from the foaming green sea. They needed no illumination other than the massive moon as they took their places on the tiers of the floating arena and waited.

Unlike the warm planet of Ojal, with its perpetual sunlight and dense atmosphere, Taigal Rax was a cool, dimly lit world. Though there was enough daylight to support its life forms, the oceans had submerged the continents long ago. The Taigalians carried water in their spacecraft as others carried atmosphere and had evolved to take their essential gases from both air and water. Once they had been green but, as they became more sophisticated, they had turned silver. Their blood was cool, so was their appearance and manner. Though not uncharitable, they were frighteningly practical.

One of the Taigalians was elevated on a pedestal lit by a phosphorescent beam to address the gathering.

'This will not take long. It is only a minor matter that needs your authorisation.' She went on to explain how their planet had transmitted an android to Perimeter 84926 for the Ojalie in order to help them trace the Star Dancer. Although designed to the most advanced standards by both planets, the android had not fulfilled its function of neutralising the creature on its planet of origin, had involved four humans with potentially disastrous results, and now refused to dismantle itself when instructed.

'Perhaps you designed it too well?' a voice from the audience suggested.

'Perhaps,' the speaker agreed. 'The unit was very advanced and able to assume any human form. The Kybion even has the potential to acquire a human biology by absorbing its original circuits.'

The audience sat in stunned silence for a moment.

Only the wind and crashing of the waves could be heard until another voice enquired, 'That means it could, in every respect, become a human being. Without us having control over it, the Kybion would then be free to do whatever it wants.'

'And that would contravene all laws of non-interference. We must have your authorisation to activate the service robots in the oceans of Perimeter 84926 to capture and destroy it,' announced the speaker.

'Isn't there any other way?'

'The only alternative is to leave it alone. Even if that were not in contravention of so many laws, we have no idea what it would get up to.'

'How powerful is it at the moment?'

'As far as we know it still has the potential built into it as an android. This it may or may not decide to retain. If it wants to assume human form completely then, naturally, it will not be able to carry those power units. This would make it much easier to catch. As soon as we have captured it, the Kybion will be scanned to discover the reason for its malfunction, and then dismantled.'

The audience chattered and nodded amongst themselves. Then they plunged into the sea and back to their homes, where they would make their decision.

As the platform lowered the speaker, she said to one of her colleagues waiting below, 'There'll be no problem with the vote. Better tell the technicians to start the signal. We can send the service robots out as soon as we have the authorisation.'

'This is going to be somewhat unpleasant,' the colleague reminded her.

'Stupid machine should have thought of that before. The Watchers would probably dismantle our orbit if they ever found out about this. No one can afford to break laws like these.'

'It might be missed by the humans who know it.'

'It cannot tell anyone on Perimeter 84926 what it is, and no human would believe it if it did. It will be a simple matter to pick the android up and dismember it without arousing any suspicion.

'All that technology. What a waste.'

***

In a station tower cooled by ocean thermals far above the water's surface, technicians lnsac, and Helto received confirmation of the speaker's authorisation and activated the signal to receivers deep in the Earth's sea.

The operatives had originally been selected for their calm reason, practical execution of duties, and inability to wonder at miracles of Nature. That was some while ago. They were both mature enough now to wonder why they had applied in the first place, especially Helto. Insac, her regular shift partner, was well aware she would rather be travelling the solar system or piecing together data from space probes. In exchange for promising not to make public his liaison with a deep ocean mineral analyst, Helto was occasionally allowed to air her unTaigalian views without fear of report.

'Only call out one at first,' Insac said. 'The Kybion must still be carrying the power units. We don't want to attract too much attention.'

'We don't want to attract any attention,' Helto reminded him. 'Those robots are grotesque. Think how

113

they would appear to a human being.'

'They wouldn't be able to stand the pressure down there if they weren't. It's the only place we can keep them out of their interfering hands.'

'Why can't we wait and see if it really has decided to create a human biology for itself? Then we would know it must eventually die of old age.'

'Because laws are laws,' said lnsac. 'We'd better make a good job of it and send in the results when we have them. We've managed this long without being investigated; let's keep it that way. Send the robot its instructions as soon as it's free of the cocoon.'

CHAPTER 16

After several days realigning her human perceptions and learning to conceal her heightened senses, Gabrielle was relieved to receive a phone call from Penny to say that she and Paula were coming home early because the weather was so foul. With only a brief visit from Weatherby in that time, Gabrielle needed someone to talk to. Although her nightmares had stopped, strange dreams now invaded her sleep. That mocking voice was calling to her from the abyss of space. She was afraid that one night she might go to it and never be able to wake up again.

As Gabrielle was paying one of her dream visits to the enigmatic artificial world where some mysterious device was being constructed, the voice called to her. This time it was distinct, almost motherly.

'Why look so hard, Star Dancer?'

Gabrielle responded like a truculent teenager. 'Don't call me that. Why shouldn't I be curious?'

'But you already know everything in this Universe, my delinquent offspring.'

'Offspring?' Gabrielle's curiosity in the artificial world evaporated. 'Who are you?'

'My name is Vian Solran.'

'But - you're the monster the Ojalie believe came from a primeval quasar?'

'Like you, I gave up all my bad habits.' The voice now had an odd, unsettling resonance. 'In fact, I not only gave them up, I became a Watcher.'

'Watcher? That sounds familiar.'

'I implement the Law. I hold my power in abeyance until called upon to use it.'

'Then who makes galactic law?'

'Us Watchers.'

Gabrielle paused. 'If you are who you say, why waste time talking to a minor astral traveller like me?'

There was a gentle, ringing laugh.

'You are my thought child. Se who had three parents.'

'Se?'

'You. Thought has no gender.'

'Then you gave me that dreadful power... but why?'

'So you would live. It was not time for you to die when your parents did. Your species needs many more like you, but so few qualify.'

'I nearly destroyed a planet.'

'Some of my offspring can be careless. They inherited that from me.'

'If I hadn't realised in time...'

'You would have done. That was why I chose you. Unlike most others, your subconscious has sense.'

'But Toby, Gunn, Mrs Tavistock, and Tasmin?'

'Mortal concerns. They no longer exist, as you knew them,' Vian Solran explained. 'I would like you to understand. Come with me.'

The strange mechanical planet faded and millions of symbols snowed about Gabrielle.

She looked at the one she already held. 'What are these?'

'They are The Law.'

The symbols parted and spiralled away.

'What does a Watcher do then?'

'We watch. Some of us watch a million worlds, some concentrate on those few viruses floating in space that can lay waste to star clusters... We watch...'

'And?'

'Seldom do anything. Each of us has the power of a supernova. Some, a quasar. Look...'

Gabrielle was aware of a small figure, apparently fast asleep, in a cushioning mist. It was young, fair, and blissfully unaware of their presence.

'Toby!' exclaimed Gabrielle.

'I have taken him from the life spiral for a short while. You told me he needed to rest.'

'I told you?'

'You tell me many things, Star Dancer. Why shouldn't you? Aren't you my child? Or would you rather see your mortal parents?'

'Where are they?'

'Look.'

Suddenly Gabrielle was gazing down from a blue sky. In a dry, rusty landscape, people crowded the edge of a wide river.

'That's India!'

'Your father believed he would be reincarnated here after he died. Shall I point him out?'

'No!' Gabrielle blurted out. 'Show me my mother.'

The Earth disappeared. Thick purple clouds enveloped them. Gabrielle was floating in the outer layers of a gaseous planet. Swimming with them were kite-winged creatures.

'Shall I point her out?' asked Vian Solran.

Gabrielle sighed. 'No.'

'What is wrong?'

'With the power you gave me, I ceased to be any mortal's child.'

'Every mortal and immortal thing is related. Come

to me again and I will explain how.'

'When?'

'You will know. Now you must answer the door.'

The teenager woke with a start to find the milkwoman wanting to know how many pints she needed. She somehow knew that Penny and Paula would be returning that day.

***

Gabrielle arrived early at the station to help her aunt carry the suitcases down to the cottage. When they arrived home she listened patiently while Penny went into the tedious details of their failed package holiday. The hotel had only been partly built, the water had to be boiled, and Paula had somehow managed to get sunburnt on the only day it stopped raining.

'You should have a suntan like mine,' Gabrielle teased her. 'You would cook more gradually then.'

Suddenly remembering her emails, Paula shot upstairs to switch on her PC.

'If she's had any more junk from that creepy pervert, I'll hide that computer,' threatened Penny.

'You should report it.'

'Why? Paula's not daft, just gets some strange pleasure in leading him on.'

Gabrielle tried not to sound shocked. 'Penny...'

'She's told him that her father's a billionaire with six daughters who all drive quad bikes. She knows more about that sad package that he'll ever find out about her.'

'All the same...'

'It's all right. I keep that one on a short lead.'

'But he could be after more gullible kids.'

'There is that, I suppose.' Penny noticed that Gabrielle looked tired. 'Has everything been all right here? You don't look that well?'

'I did have a rather unpleasant surprise.'

Penny was immediately concerned. 'Why? What's happened, Gabby?'

'Well,' Gabrielle started carefully, knowing she would have to tell her something, though unsure how much. 'A policeman phoned to say he would be popping in later today.' Penny's jaw dropped, 'It's all right. I'm not in trouble of any sort. It's just that I was the last person to see that strange blond man who lived in the bungalow before he was killed in a fire.'

'My God!' Penny sat down, clutching the shoe and bottle of eau de Cologne she had been unpacking.

'Did you know him?'

'No... No. It's just that nothing's ever happened around here since Albert Cooney ran through the village wearing nothing but a union jack and plastic bucket, screaming that Napoleon was coming. It took half a dozen nurses to catch him.'

'Oh, Mr Wendle was killed some way from here,' Gabrielle explained. 'I met him on top of the cliff and we got chatting. They say he never used to talk to anyone. I suppose they think he might have told me something useful.'

'What a thing.' Penny shook her head. 'He was a strange one, I know, but he never did harm to anyone.' She paused. 'Are you sure everything else is all right?'

'Of course.' Gabrielle laughed. 'As long as you don't mind this detective coming here. He's a bit of a character - but really quite nice,' she added, hoping Weatherby wouldn't go and blab out any more than she had told Penny.

'Well, we'd better tidy up then.' Penny jumped to her feet. 'What time's he coming?'

'Oh, don't rush about because of him,' Gabrielle told her. 'He's only a copper.'

'But I've not had a policeman here since I had to call them out over...' She glanced about to make sure Paula wasn't eavesdropping. 'Frank coming back to cause trouble after the divorce.'

Oh yes, even Gabrielle could remember that strangely sinister, dull man at a cousin's wedding, and wondering why such a lively person as Penny would have married him. She really needed someone with a sense of humour and open nature, not a nondescript sociopath. Having spent her impressionable years with a father like that could account for why Paula enjoyed tormenting inadequate men.

Gabrielle helped Penny unpack and put the clothes to be laundered in the washing machine. Then she cooked a meal for the three of them. By the time Weatherby knocked at the cottage door, she felt too tired to answer it. It didn't matter; Penny was there before he had the opportunity to snatch a glance through the letterbox. Rearranging her light brown hair and snatching off her apron, she swung the front door open to look straight at a bright, satin, paisley waistcoat. Penny was stunned for a second by Weatherby's striking appearance, and wouldn't have said anything if he hadn't introduced himself.

'Come in, come in.' Penny suddenly found her warm smile and escorted him into the living room where Gabrielle lay sprawled out in an armchair, and Paula sat moping in a corner with her sunburn.

Gabrielle lifted a hand in salute. At the sight of the tall black detective in the fancy waistcoat, Paula stopped moping and became interested.

'Mr Weatherby,' Penny said, as though Gabrielle might not recognise him.

Weatherby beamed. 'Hello.'

Penny scuttled off to the kitchen to bring in the tea tray.

'Hello stranger.' Gabrielle brought a finger to her lips to tell him to be careful what he said.

'I've brought something you might be interested in.' Weatherby took an envelope from his inside pocket and waved it tantalisingly.

Gabrielle wasn't sure how to react. She was becoming convinced that the man was a good deal brighter than she had originally given him credit for.

Gabrielle pointed to the ten-year-old. 'The sunburned kid is Paula, by the way.'

He smiled. 'Hi.'

Paula cast him an analytical gaze. 'I get emails from a pervert.'

Weatherby gritted his teeth. 'That so?'

'I think he lives in Birmingham, but they all lie, don't they.'

'Don't pay any attention,' said Gabriel. 'She's winding you up because he hasn't sent any mail since she's been away. Come and sit down.'

Instead of going to the armchair she indicated, Weatherby tipped the contents of the envelope onto the table.

Gabrielle saw a latchkey drop out and joined him. 'What's that?'

'I received this several days ago. I couldn't say anything about it to you then because I had to contact the solicitor and make sure it was all above board. She's apparently received the same instructions as well.'

'What is it?' Gabrielle tried to sneak a page of the document away from him.

'He must have made his mind up about this while you two were -' Weatherby stopped as he felt the hot breath of a curious Paula peering over his shoulder.

'Why don't you go and print out all the correspondence that pervert's been sending you, and let me have it?'

'It's private.'

'So is this.'

'Ignore her. Why not just tell me?' Gabrielle pleaded.

'Mr Wendle left you his bungalow.'

Paula shrieked with excitement and ran into the kitchen, 'Mum! Mum! Gabby's been left a house!'

Taking the opportunity of her brief absence, Gabrielle hissed across the table to Weatherby, 'They only know I talked to Mr Wendle before he died. Nothing else.'

'All right.' Weatherby gave her one of his more perceptive smiles. 'How are you feeling now?'

'Shattered.'

'I'm not surprised.'

'I'm beginning to dream about creatures called Watchers and symbols called Law.'

The smile fell from his face as though ice had been poured down his back, 'Watchers..?' Before he could say any more, Paula returned with Penny and tea tray in hot pursuit.

'I don't believe it!' Penny exclaimed. She thrust the tray on to the table and nearly concealed the evidence.

'It's true.' Weatherby refixed his smile. 'I've checked with the solicitor. Mr Wendle made her this deed of gift and sent a copy to me. The only problem was, it hadn't been witnessed, but it's been authenticated with a specimen signature. With no one to contest the gift, it looks as though you have acquired property.' He saw that Gabrielle's mixed emotions made it difficult for her to say anything. 'He also left you an endowment so you could afford to keep the place, pay the council tax, et cetera.'

Gabrielle was unsure what to think. 'Is that what he wanted?'

'It wasn't a condition, though he expressed the wish that you should.'

'That would be ideal for you. Gabrielle,' Penny joined in. 'Even if you didn't live there all the year round, it would make you independent.'

'And I could come and stay with you,' Paula

reminded her.

'Now don't go and turn it down.' Weatherby looked straight at her. 'It's what he wanted. He must have thought he owed you something. It'll only go to the government otherwise.'

'Silly man,' Gabrielle murmured. 'What do you think?'

'Take it.' He laid his hand on the back of hers. 'Here's the latchkey. All you need do is visit the solicitor before you go inside.'

As Weatherby and Gabrielle talked, Penny absently held the teapot and watched the detective intently. A drop of scalding tea fell onto her foot, yet she remained transfixed. Eventually, the teapot became too hot to hold any longer. 'Milk and sugar?'

'No sugar for me, Penny,' Gabrielle said.

'Mr Weatherby?'

'No thank you. I had one not so long ago. I won't be keeping you any longer anyway.'

'That's all right. I was going into town to collect a few things, but it's a bit late now. I'll have to leave it until tomorrow.'

'I can give you a lift in if you like?' Weatherby offered.

Penny's face lit up. 'Could you really?'

'Can I come too, Mum?' Paula demanded, also fascinated by Weatherby, and the chance of a ride in a police car.

'No. You stop here with Gabrielle. I won't be long.'

Leaving Gabrielle to watch over the bored ten-year-old with sunburn, Weatherby drove Penny into town.

The policeman was blissfully unaware that the divorcee found him attractive and, like a homely cat, was becoming more and more intrigued by his friendly diffidence. By the end of the journey, Penny was totally hooked. All Weatherby had to do was reel her in, assuming he could find the data for that sort of angling.

'Are you sure Gabrielle isn't in some sort of trouble?' Penny asked Weatherby anxiously as they got out of the car. 'This business of being left a bungalow seems odd to me.'

'Oh, Mr Wendle had no relatives. There won't be any disputes about its ownership.'

'It was very quick though. She's only been here a few days.'

Weatherby hesitated for a moment, unable to think up other reassurance, and because he was oddly reluctant to part company with her. 'Why don't we find somewhere to talk?' he suggested.

Penny promptly forgot shopping and leapt at the idea. She knew just the quiet corner teashop for a tête-à-tête.

'I owed Mr Wendle a small favour for his help with my enquiries and agreed to be his executor,' Weatherby told Penny over the chrome silver tea service and wheatmeal biscuits. 'Gabrielle just happened to be the last person to see him alive. We think he may have been murdered, but she's not implicated in any way.'

Penny gasped. 'Murdered! She's not in any sort of danger?'

'Goodness no.'

'Only, it's that I don't want her parents to worry. My brother and his wife are so fond of Gabrielle. It would break their hearts if anything happened to her. She's such a gentle and bright girl. We all think the world of her.'

Bright, certainly. But gentle? It was obvious none of the family knew how tough she really was.

'Yes, she does seem like a bright girl. Perhaps Mr Wendle wanted to give her the opportunity to do things she wouldn't have otherwise been able to?'

'That might be true. Jack and Connie have never been well off since he was made redundant two years ago. Though they're hoping she'll go to university. She needs to know the results of her exams before deciding which one.' Penny smiled. 'I am really glad for her, Mr Weatherby. Gabrielle deserves to have a decent chance. She's the only one in the family with any brains. I sometimes think my Paula is going to end up in a shoe shop or as a clerk in the town hall with me.'

Penny's bright eyes couldn't conceal her glumness at the prospect, and Weatherby laughed.

'Well, there's still time to raise an Einstein,' he reassured her.

Penny burst out laughing and the other customers turned to see what the joke was.

'Another child at my age, Mr Weatherby,' she managed to whisper as she became aware of the attention she had attracted, 'I'm forty-four and divorced.'

Weatherby shrugged at his faux pas, though remained convinced that human females were still able to breed at that age.

'How old did you think I was?'

He grinned in false embarrassment. 'Much younger than me.'

'How old are you, then?' she asked mischievously.

'Something like that,' he replied secretively.

'Really, Mr Weatherby, fancy being ashamed to admit your age,' she teased, and patted the back of his hand.

At her touch, Weatherby felt all manner of unfamiliar feelings flooding through his highly co-ordinated body. He had thought her pretty face framed by brown hair interesting. Now something unfathomable was interfering with his circuits, and he began to worry that he was malfunctioning in some way. Worse still, Penny seemed to be having the same reaction, and he was sure she understood what it was all about.

***

Next day, after signing the solicitor's papers, Gabrielle took Paula along the cliff to show her the bungalow. She didn't stay long or let her touch anything. The teenager was still uneasy about the bequest and tried to pluck up the courage to spend a night there.

When they returned to the cottage, Penny was on the phone. Paula dashed out into the back garden. Gabrielle went into the living room, slumped into an armchair, and picked up the heavy volume she had borrowed from the library. Flicking through the pages to find the place Paula had lost for her, she overheard Penny talking in the hall.

'What do you mean?' her aunt was saying. 'Yes, I know you're a racist turd, but that still doesn't make it any business of yours... Don't be so idiotic. The man's a policeman, so don't think about starting trouble!' She slammed the receiver down and marched into the kitchen.

Gabrielle momentarily lost interest in her book. This was more intriguing than Napoleonic campaigns. She decided to stay in for the rest of the day, waiting for the gentle knock at the front door, and Paula's piercing tones shrieking, 'Hello, Mr Weatherby. Mum's in the garden and Gabby's in the living room.'

Gabrielle knew that the detective hadn't come to see her and heard his footsteps going down the side passage, into the garden.

Penny tried her best to appear surprised at seeing him, yet barely succeeded. Although pulling weeds in the garden, she was wearing one of her best dresses and eye make-up.

Weatherby took a pair of white gloves from his pocket. 'You left these in the teashop. I was passing so

125

I thought I'd drop them in.'

'Didn't think you ever wore them, Mum,' Paula commented in a very loud voice, and was promptly told to go and play with her pervert.

When her bright red shorts and ponytail were out of sight, Penny said, 'That's very kind of you, Mr Weatherby. I'm sure you needn't have bothered.'

'I had some free time. Things are very slack at the moment. It's the time of year you see. With no tourists in these parts and everyone going on holiday... things are very quiet,' he was running out of data for small talk.

'Yes, it is...' Penny was obviously having the same problem. 'It's not very often we get visitors here.' She was unable to keep up the sophisticated front any longer and the smile suddenly faded.

'What's wrong?'

Penny stood awkwardly fluttering her hands. She didn't want to tell him, but blurted out despite herself, 'It's my ex-husband, Frank - He saw us together yesterday and jumped to the wrong conclusion.'

'Why worry about that?'

'I had to divorce him because he was so jealous. Then he was always watching me until the police stepped in. He saw us yesterday by chance and phoned this morning to warn me to keep away from you.'

Weatherby laughed. 'He can't do that. He'll be having more trouble with the police if he keeps that up.' He put his arm reassuringly round her shoulders, much to the delight of Gabrielle and Paula who were watching from the French windows.

'I'm worried, Mr Weatherby. It's not as if you're just any man...' She stopped awkwardly, waiting for him to take the point. For some reason the hint didn't register, so Penny went on, 'I mean, he still regards me as his property and never accepted the divorce. I sometimes think he's a little mad.'

'If he gives you any trouble you must phone me right away,' Weatherby released her to write down some telephone numbers in his notebook. 'This one is the station, this one my flat, and that's my mobile.' He tore out the page and handed it to her.

He was about to replace his arm about her shoulders, then glimpsed the grinning faces at the French windows and changed his mind.

'My Frank always was a bit narrow-minded. In fact he was born believing he was the only one made in God's image. Once he pulled a knife on a man the same colour as you just because he looked at him the wrong way.' Penny managed to hold Weatherby's hand without the audience seeing. 'He might try to harm you as well.' He laughed vigorously at the idea. 'You may be a policeman, but if he's got murder on his mind, that won't stop him.'

'I'm sorry. Seems as though we'd better be careful if we want to meet each other again then.'

'Yes. We'd better be careful. There is one thing though.'

'What's that?'

'I'd like to know your Christian name?'

Weatherby was stumped for a moment.

'Well,' he hedged. 'My parents weren't Christian.'

CHAPTER 17

Gabrielle eventually decided to spend the night in Wendle's bungalow.

Everything she needed was there, from immaculately laundered bedclothes to long life milk. Not needing to supply her niece with any essentials made Penny feel superfluous, as though a dead man had usurped her familial position.

When Paula had finished exploring the bungalow and left, Gabrielle wound the grandfather clock, and

sat quietly until it chimed ten o'clock, then went to bed
to read about Napoleon and poisonous wallpaper. She
soon fell asleep.

That night Vian Solran took her to a nebulous
temple at the centre of the Galaxy. It was formed from
the tattered remains of a star shredded by a black hole
with an impossible disregard for gravity.

'Why are we here?' Gabrielle asked.

Vian Solran turned to the collapsar's event
horizon. 'On the other side of that dimension is my
parent. Your grandparent. Would you like to see her,
Star Dancer?'

'What? In a black hole?'

'Come with me.'

The temple's strands of star matter unravelled and
Gabrielle felt herself being drawn into infinity after
them. Though she was only there in thought, she
almost panicked at the idea of not being able to get
back.

'No parent like us would harm their offspring,'
Vian Solran reassured her.

With a sudden explosion of light, they were
spinning in a dazzling new universe. Gabrielle turned
to see they had been ejected from a quasar.

'Into a black hole, and out of a quasar,' said Vian
Solran. 'My parent turned inside out. We can be born
as many times as we like.'

'How can a quasar be anyone's parent?'

'Quasars are the parents of us all.'

'But has it intelligence?'

Vian Solran laughed. 'When you are a quasar, you
do not need intelligence... You are.'

This dimension was young and alight with glowing
clouds giving birth to stars. For aeons there would be
no night here. Gabrielle may have been a Star Dancer,
but this vibrant dimension was overpowering. She
slipped out of her dream sweating with relief.

The next morning, Gabrielle dusted the only ornaments in the sparsely furnished living room, and again wondered who could have tidied up the place.

Taking the brief walk into the village, she couldn't avoid meeting Dot. The woman seemed to have radar that let her know when the student was coming. Gabrielle knew it would only be a matter of time before she found out she had been left the bungalow, so decided to tell her before the gossips got round to it.

Dot was thrilled at getting the news before anyone else. The fact that the property had gone to a total newcomer didn't seem to cross her mind. Dot's curiosity had no side to it, and she wasn't mercenary enough to wonder what Gabrielle had done to deserve it. Others would get round to that soon enough.

'There's a thing... I suppose you must know that black man who went in there the other day then?'

Weatherby. Gabrielle laughed at herself for not associating him with the tidy bungalow. Of course, he would have had to visit it to search for any clues. It would have been just like him to lift a DNA a sample, and then forget to lock the door.

'Oh, he's a police detective,' she was surprised that Dot didn't already know. 'He's been investigating the case.'

'Strange fellow he is.'

Gabrielle found herself defending him. She had no idea why; perhaps telling her that she had been left a bungalow had something to do with it. 'He's all right. He's been pretty good over this business.'

'No, I didn't mean that.'

Gabrielle wondered what was so odd about him that she didn't already know. 'What then?'

'One of the lads was setting lobster pots in the cove late the other evening and reckoned he saw him walking along the beach.'

'If you can walk the on pebbles round here without

ricking your ankles, I don't see the harm in that?'

'But he was in Wrecker's Cove,' Dot told her. 'The only way you can get down there is by the sea.'

'He must have found a boat from somewhere, or clambered down somehow.' The idea amused Gabrielle. 'He's a determined sort of fellow.'

'Not very likely. There was no dinghy. The lad saw him walk round the rocks and disappear from sight.'

Gabrielle felt uncomfortable. This was something she would have preferred not to know but, having found out so much, asked, 'How far is the cove from the town?'

'Oh, not too far from Smuggler's Halt, though the safest way to reach it is to take a bus into town then go the long way round.'

'Why is it called Wrecker's Cove if wreckers couldn't reach the shore to get to the shipwrecked cargo?'

Dot laughed. 'Well, you're a sharp one and no mistake. County Council renamed it. Used to be called Stinkweed Bay. It don't have that trouble since the sea level rose. That's what cut it off.'

'How far is Wrecker's Cove from the town?'

'Oh,' Dot scratched the mole on her chin, 'about a mile and a half as the crow flies.'

Gabrielle was amazed. 'Is that all?'

'Can't be any more. There's no public coast road because no one much lives along there, only recluses and wealthy boat owners. And that land's private. They don't take kindly to trespassers.'

'I never realised the town was that close to the sea,' murmured Gabrielle. The tunnel she had walked through was less than half a kilometre. Things were beginning to make horrible sense.

'You want to go up there and have a look, don't you?'

'How dangerous is it along the top of the cliffs?'

'Well, don't choose a blowy day or you'll be swept off.'

'When's low tide?'

'Couple of hours,' Then Dot warned sternly, 'Now don't you go trying to get down there. The place is a death trap. More people have been lost along that stretch than get parking tickets around here. It should really be fenced off.'

'All right,' agreed Gabrielle. 'I promise.'

Later that morning she started out. As she climbed up the public path that ran up from the beach the wind whistled furiously as though it hated every inch of the cliffs. Gabrielle trudged on into the teeth of the gale and was relieved when she reached the top of Wrecker's Cove. She laid flat and peered over the sheer walls to a semi-circular patch of shingle beach. There was no way down, and no access from the adjoining beaches at low tide. For some distance, the top of the cliffs were desolate, rock strewn and pitted, and too unstable for buildings. Behind her, the picaresque hills were peppered with mansions, chalets, and villas.

Gabrielle wanted to believe that there was some simple explanation for Weatherby's apparent ability to walk under water, other than the one that kept springing to her mind. That would have explained how he had tracked her down to the caverns that day, how he had managed to walk out of a blazing house, and why Wendle had been so anxious she should leave. Yet it didn't explain why Weatherby hadn't killed her to prevent the destruction of an alien world. That was the only reason he could have been sent. Gabrielle shuddered at the thought. She didn't want to believe he was the missing Kybion, especially as Penny had taken such a fancy to him and, impossibly, him to her. Could an android fall in love?

Gabrielle turned back down the cliffs, too deep in thought to register that she was walking against a furious wind that had somehow managed to change direction and fight her as hard as it did on the way up there.

CHAPTER 18

The pebbles rattled and cracked as the creature put down immense feet and made its ponderous way up the shore. The huge monster's body was squat and wide and had several pairs of snake-like arms that could retract into its body when not needed. Its skin was grey and slimy and left a trail on whatever it touched. There was no face in the human sense of the word, just a wide, flat head that joined the shoulders, with a lateral slit running around it. A light inside the slit flashed and occasionally sent out an intense beam that illuminated the beach with a sickly green light as it searched.

The mechanical kraken was unsure of what direction to take its stroll in the moonlight and emitted a high frequency sound that excited the cats and dogs in Smuggler's Halt half a mile away as it tried to locate a particular brain signal. Having no success, it moved a little further up the shore and repeated the process several times. Finally it was standing before a large bungalow laid out like a Roman villa. The creature deduced that there was nothing substantial enough in its way to prevent it from investigating further and moved through the villa - without opening the door.

Fortunately the place was empty; this sea monster hardly had the stealth of a cat burglar. Without a signal to follow, it blundered into pillars and furniture, eventually achieving the height of bad manners by walking through the far wall and out into the night air again.

The monster's scanner evidently didn't have the range required, so it turned around, lumbered back through the villa and down to the waves licking the pebble beach.

Insac and Helto had been watching the tachyon signal transmitted by the robot in their tower control on Taigal Rax.

'Not exactly delicate workers, are they?' Helto observed. 'Just as well we only sent one.'

Insac had a solution to everything. 'It'll never be able to run after anything. We'll have to widen its scan.'

'I don't envy the Kybion when one of those robots gets its tentacles on it.'

'Stop thinking about that. It's not our job to make moral judgements.'

'Then we must be the only ones on this planet without that privilege.' Helto fluttered her dorsal fin in annoyance. 'The problem with interfering in other planets' affairs is that there's always a price to pay to protect them from the consequences. Those humans probably wouldn't be affected it we did leave the android down there.'

'Laws are laws,' lnsac reminded her. 'We wouldn't be able to go anywhere if we didn't keep to them. I've never heard of a Watcher blasting a planet from its orbit, but it would only take one of them a nanosecond to do it.'

'Then Controller Opu should be taking some of the blame for this.'

'Maybe. We just happen to be closer.'

Helto stretched her fins. 'Oh. I'm going for a swim.'

'Well, remember to close the lower hatch when you come back,' lnsac reminded her. 'We don't want the place flooding again.'

'Why not? All that salt's good for you.'

'It isn't for the equipment. Why do you think they build places this high?'

Helto laughed at her serious partner. 'So they can

touch the stars.' She opened the tower hatch and plunged into the cool green depths below.

***

The Clarke Johnsons were returning late that night from their friends, the Rosenbergs, to their villa overlooking the sea. As the car entered the private road that served six other remote bungalows at Heron's Point as well as their own, Mrs Clarke Johnson had one of her forebodings. The Major paid little attention. She had been having foreboding feelings regularly every other night for the past twenty-four years. It wasn't until he drove past the smashed gateposts, and the car's headlights picked out the massive hole in the masonry that he was inclined to believe her.

Being an ex-soldier, he wasn't going to be intimidated by an intruder, even ones that demolished the sides of villas. Despite Mrs Clarke Johnson's insistence that he call the police first, the gallant Major sprang out of the car to take the culprit unawares. As not only the door had been dismantled, but a good deal of the wall it had been attached to as well, his bravado was somewhat futile.

Once inside, he turned on the nearest light switch and saw the large pits in the floorboards running through the wreckage of their home. They ended at the hole he had seen from the outside of the villa. Even he was staggered and his military poise briefly visited Fairyland.

He was startled by the sound of his wife shrieking, 'Call the police, quickly!'

The Major was still listening to Mustardseed and Peaseblossom giggling in the tinkling of the smashed chandelier as it swayed in the breeze. 'Eh - what?'

'Oh, never mind.' Seeing that her husband wasn't going to be much use, she broke into a state of sudden calmness and made the call herself.

Two whiskies and two gins later, they heard the sound of a police car arriving quietly in their drive. It hadn't even bothered to put its siren down. Where was the point in having a major incident if the neighbours didn't know about it? Had he been totally sober, the retired soldier would have recalled that he was the one always ranting on about noise nuisance in the neighbourhood.

The irate Major charged out before the police constable and detective could open the doors of the car.

'What kept you, man?' he boomed.

'Private roads not on maps are difficult to find in the dark, sir,' called Weatherby. 'They need lighting of some sort. Flashing lights would have probably helped, but I understand they're prohibited hereabouts. Might have helped if you'd caught fire as well.'

The young policewoman gazed at her superior with a mixture of admiration and apprehension.

'I manage all right,' declared the ex-soldier with twenty years of military service and a good deal of whisky in his tone.

Then Detective Inspector Weatherby got out of the car.

The outraged Major stared at the tall plain-clothes detective in the fancy waistcoat and his pert uniformed companion who looked as though she had just been transferred from the Girl Scouts. 'Is there only the two of you?' He turned on his heels and strode back inside in disgust.

'That's right, sir,' replied Weatherby as he and his teenage colleague bounced and trotted respectively after him, over the fallen front door and masonry that had once surrounded it. 'But the most efficient available.'

The Major jabbed a thumb in the direction of the lady swaying to and fro on a high stool at the cocktail bar. 'Me wife. She should be in bed, but there's a draught coming through the hole in the bedroom wall.'

'Hole?' asked Weatherby.

The Major pointed towards the end of the trail of destruction.

'Mice around here seem to be a bit neurotic,' Weatherby observed. Seeing the Major didn't have a sense of humour, especially at that moment, he pulled out his notebook. 'When did this happen, Mr..?'

'Major. Major Clarke Johnson. And I haven't the faintest idea.'

Weatherby caught sight of the slimy trail running along the walls and hall carpet. 'I think we need to call forensics out on this.'

'You can do what you like,' announced Mrs Clarke Johnson swaying off the stool and tottering round the holes in the floor to the phone, 'but I am going back to the Rosenbergs for the night.'

'I don't think it would be wise for you to drive in that state, ma'am,' Weatherby warned her, but she was already talking on the phone. 'Call Forensics and take Mrs Clarke Johnson wherever she wants, Perkins,' he told the policewoman. He turned to the Major. 'Do you want to go with your wife, sir - I mean Major?'

'No chance. I'm staying here,' he snorted as though he trusted Weatherby even less that the nocturnal bulldozer that had trashed his home.

When Perkins returned with the car, a couple of sleepy forensic experts were taking samples and photographs of anything particularly obnoxious-looking inside the bungalow. Weatherby and his young colleague made their way down to the shore with flashlights.

'Do you believe in sea monsters, Perkins?' he asked.

She looked at the massive indentations in the

pebble beach where the shingle had been impacted. 'I do now, sir. You can't pin this one on the mice.'

'Doesn't it bother you?' Weatherby stooped to measure one of the depressions.

'I would guess from the size and depth of these footprints, that whatever made them would be pretty clumsy. It's probably drunk as well,' she mused thoughtfully. 'I think I could easily outrun one of them.'

That wasn't the reply he'd been after. 'They must mean something to you other than stopwatch mathematics and breathalysers?'

'What's that, sir?' the keen young woman enquired.

'It's all bloody terrifying!' he blurted out so suddenly he surprised himself.

'I never thought of you as the type to get scared, sir. After all, there's probably a quite rational explanation for it.'

'Tell me one, Perkins?' Weatherby pleaded, becoming aware of one of his own.

She smiled sweetly up at him. 'Oh, I'm sure you you'll be able to work it out. After all, you usually do, don't you?' Then the pint sized, over-enthusiastic Perkins bounded back to the bungalow as another constable beckoned to her.

Weatherby slumped onto the pebble beach and, resting his chin on his knees, flickered his torch idly over the trail of depressions before him. Meeting Penny had kindled one human emotion in him, and now this outrageous amount of evidence was fanning another into life. It sent a chill of mortal terror through him. He had been over-optimistic in thinking Taigal Rax could do nothing about him deciding on android liberation. The slimy something that had lumbered from the depths of the sea had undoubtedly been sent to track him. Destroying the unpleasant Major's villa was just a fortunate diversion.

Jutting out his chin thoughtfully, Weatherby
wondered why he was sitting there in full range of the
robot as though he wanted to be carried off and
dissected. Even the unfriendly Major was preferable, so
he got up and returned to the bungalow.

'Well?' snapped the retired soldier as soon as he
walked in over the door.

'Oh,' said Weatherby absently, 'we'll rehang the door
for you - if we can find the doorposts, and put tarpaulins
over the holes.'

'I meant, who d'you think did it?' the Major
bellowed, nearly treading on one of the forensic men
collecting specimens from a hole in the floor in his haste
to pursue the detective into the living room.

'Well,' said Weatherby thoughtfully, 'it's not mice.
Whatever came through here wasn't after cheese.'

'You, sir,' barked the Major, 'Are a fool! It no doubt
goes with your complexion.'

Weatherby rubbed his chin thoughtfully. 'But then,'
he mused, 'it might have been a rat.'

CHAPTER 19

The next morning, Weatherby was inside the cavern
under the cliffs trying to raise Taigal Rax. It was more
difficult this time. They obviously saw no point in
talking to him any more. When something eventually
appeared on the screen, the picture didn't come into
focus and an irate voice snapped, 'This channel should
be closed. Transmission must cease.'

'I've got to talk to someone,' Weatherby pleaded.
'You can't all have seaweed in your ears.'

'The decision has been made. Nothing can
countermand it.'

'No wait!' Weatherby called before the faint image
could disappear. 'Can't we come to some arrangement?'

'I do not have the power to make agreements.' And

the transmission went dead.

Weatherby left the channel open in the desperate hope that someone on Taigal Rax would relent. After several minutes a different channel opened, and a shimmering individual with white-edged silver scales appeared.

'Hello, little android,' Helto said. 'Why are you trying to contact us now?'

'I saw the mess one of your service robots made of a bungalow,' Weatherby admitted. 'And I've been thinking about the sort of mess it's a liable to make when it catches me.'

'You had the chance to dismantle yourself. You still can if you haven't started to develop a human biology.' From Weatherby's silence it was obvious that he had. 'When did you make that decision?'

'I met an attractive woman...' Weatherby started to explain, then thought better of it.

'You can't fall in love with a human.'

'Well, I just did. Ask the ones who designed me whether it's possible or not. My power units will soon be absorbed and I'll be as human as she is.'

Helto, like everyone else, hadn't taken into account that universal free will could extend to androids. 'You didn't really think you would be allowed to do that, did you?'

'I didn't think you'd get so touchy about it if I did.'

'Stop the process before it goes too far and dismantle yourself.'

'I don't want to. Why should I?'

'Because one way or another, you have to be destroyed. That's the law. I would rather you did it your way. Please be sensible. You were constructed to be rational, even though you have avoided it up to now. The technicians have to find out what went wrong. That would mean an internal scan and could be unpleasant for a unit as sophisticated as you.'

'Well, how could I destroy an energy source without being programmed to kill the girl possessing it?' Weatherby demanded. 'Was that rational?'

'But you killed the other three humans.'

'They were already dead. I just deactivated them.'

Helto had to stop for a moment. She was beginning to wish she hadn't opened the transmission.

'Please do as I say, otherwise the service robots will have to fetch you,' she said finally.

Before Weatherby could protest, the screen went dead.

He sank to the floor and rocked backwards and forwards, deep in thought. The screen was really dead this time - and so was he.

Without warning a familiar voice demanded, 'Weatherby - How could you?'

Wrapped up in his own despondency, he nearly jumped out of his skin. A furious Gabrielle was glaring down at him. She had given him a fright that more than equalled the ones he had inflicted on her.

'Touché.'

'How could you deceive poor Penny like that?' Gabrielle accused. 'How can I tell the woman she's fallen in love with a machine? She's got all the household appliances she needs, and what sort of mechanic does she call out when you break down?'

Weatherby knew it would be useless to try and bluff his way out of this. 'I like being a living thing. I wouldn't deceive Penny for anything.'

'Then you're a muddle-minded machine with a mortality fixation! You can't fall in love with a human!'

'She finds me attractive.'

'Well, of course she does. She wouldn't have spent so much time with you if it didn't. Haven't you any sense at all? Why couldn't you have done something useful, like raking the Goodwin Sands level, or skimming up a couple of oil slicks?'

Weatherby could tell by Gabrielle's expression there was no point in trying to negotiate, so he confessed, 'My android circuits are capable of developing living tissue if so instructed - and that's what I instructed them to do. Soon my power units will be absorbed and I'll become as human as you are.'

'How could you?' scoffed Gabrielle. 'I was never an android.'

'No, you became a Star Dancer instead.'

'I didn't choose to.'

'I didn't choose to be an android. I wouldn't be here if it wasn't for you.'

'So, now it's all my fault? Do you think I enjoyed finding out what I was?'

'Why should I have any opinions? I'm only an android.'

Gabrielle sighed and had to admit. 'All right. I know you saved my life, but when you have so much power, why do you need to become human?'

'I like the way it feels. It's comfortable to have sensations flowing through you. You've always had them, so you take them for granted.'

'You've only come across the better ones so far,' Gabrielle warned. 'There are quite a few you will regret having. Have you felt fear, pain, or anger yet?'

'I've an idea I'm about to get the hang of those quite soon.'

'What do you mean?'

Weatherby laid his trench coat on the stone floor and invited her to sit beside him. Gabrielle looked at it objectively. If she accepted, there would be no going back to indignation. To her surprise, she found it no longer mattered anyway and sat down beside him.

Weatherby cast his guilty gaze at the floor. 'I should have dismantled myself after you restored the Ojalie's energy, but I didn't want to. The planet that transmitted me here has to keep within the laws about androids and what they do on other planets. They're afraid I'm going to break all of them. They've activated some service robots on the sea floor to come after me.'

'What will they do?'

'You really don't want to know.'

'It's that unpleasant?'

'The robots are already here. Yesterday I went to one of those pretentious villas at Heron's Point. One of them had walked straight through it. As soon as they get their eyesight fixed, they'll be able to pull me to them as easily as Mr Wendle was dragged to that house. So I won't be bothering you or Penny much longer.'

'What will you tell Penny?' demanded Gabrielle. 'You can't leave her believing that you might come back some day.'

'I'll think of something. I've still got some time before my power units are absorbed.'

Despite her heightened perceptions, Gabrielle wasn't able to comprehend the mixed emotions going through Weatherby. Reluctantly fascinated, she lifted her hand to feel his hair, and satin smooth skin slightly roughened by a day's growth of beard.

'How on earth could all this be so realistic - And why choose that body? And the waistcoats? It was bound to attract attention.'

'So what's wrong with attracting attention? The other camouflage options were pretty insipid.'

'Oh... vanity.' A thought suddenly occurred to Gabrielle. 'You can't have children, can you?'

'No. I've only got the equipment, not the fuel.'

'If you believe you have the right to become human, why weren't you programmed to procreate?'

'I don't know,' Weatherby confessed.

'It's because you aren't really capable of developing into a true human, isn't it?'

Weatherby said nothing. Until it actually

happened, he couldn't be sure. 'Give me a few more days,' he asked.

'What could I do about it anyway? Tell Penny you're an android from another planet sent to blow me up for stealing energy from the other side of the Galaxy? She nearly fell over when I told her about Mr Wendle being killed.'

'Once my power units are gone, I can't do anything about the robots. Then I'll be gone forever, I promise.'

'Why don't you just dismantle yourself?' Gabrielle didn't realise how sick he was of the question.

'Why do you have to be so tough?' Weatherby complained.

'Perhaps it has something to do with survival.'

'So there's your answer.'

'Oh, all right. I won't tell Penny any dreadful stories to put her off you. Even young Paula's taken a fancy to you for some reason. I don't want to be the one to shatter their illusions.'

'Thanks. I'll keep to my side of the bargain, I promise. I suppose I should be grateful I'm soon going to have the cure for my bad dreams.'

Gabrielle was surprised. 'You dream?'

'Sure. Just as I was beginning to get some interesting ones about Penny, infernal creatures with big feet and decomposing complexions started trampling through them. You can't tell me you haven't had any bad dreams lately?'

'No. They stopped when I discovered what was happening.'

'You sound guilty about something.'

'Do I?' Gabrielle got up. 'Let me know when your power units run down.' Before he could reply she left, wearing a secretive smile that added to his unease.

***

Paula and one of her friends were having a water

battle over Weatherby's car in front of Penny's cottage later that day instead of cleaning it in a more conventional manner. Penny and Weatherby sat in the cool of the living room talking about anything and everything except the way they felt about each other. Penny wasn't going to rush Weatherby to the registrar, only to discover later that he had some mental glitch like her first husband. The phone call she had received from Frank that morning was still fresh in her mind. This time his threats were delivered so calmly she had felt scared enough to phone Weatherby.

'We could have him picked up and warned,' he suggested.

Penny knew better. 'That would only make him worse. The man's already paranoid.'

'Perhaps if we weren't to see each other for a little while?' Weatherby proposed carefully.

'Oh no. While I've got time off and you're not that busy it would be foolish.' Penny added carefully, 'You don't want to stop seeing me, do you?'

'God, no!' Weatherby protested before realising he could have used the opportunity to keep his side of the bargain with Gabrielle. 'I never want to stop seeing you... but...'

'But what, Weatherby?'

'I may have to go away soon. I don't know when. I'll tell you as soon as I do.'

Penny's spirits were dampened by the news. She fidgeted with the knitting on her lap, and then suddenly announced, 'I think I'll just make a cup of tea.' She went out and called, 'I'm making a cup of tea!' into the garden through the open front door. 'Do you and Angela want one?'

'Yes please,' Paula's high-pitched voice screeched back. The soaking ten-year-old dashed into the room to give Weatherby a quick hug before following her mother and Angela into the kitchen. He could feel everything he was learning to appreciate becoming a pleasant reverie he would soon be woken from. Perhaps these were the dreams androids had, and reality was only for genuine mortals.

CHAPTER 20

Despite Weatherby's better sense telling him to stay well clear of the coast, the enthusiastic Perkins insisted on driving him out to the next sighting of slimy creatures from the deep. The detective started to have the uneasy feeling that she expected him to clear up the mystery within a few days. Having a fan as well as a lover did nothing to ease his anxiety, and he was beginning to value Gabrielle's cool disregard to help him keep his sense of proportion.

By the nearness of this sighting, it was obvious that the robots were on the right track. Although it was possible for their signal to be tuned into any part of the UK to track him down, he still preferred to be on the other side of it. Of course, the country just had to be an island surrounded by plenty of water for them to lumber from.

There was a cheerful voice at his elbow. 'Are you all right, sir?'

Weatherby was aware that the car had stopped jolting over the rough ground and he looked at Perkins.

She was watching him with unnerving expectation. 'We're there.'

'Oh yes,' he noted. 'So we are.'

They stepped out onto the rock-strewn wasteland beyond Smuggler's Halt and stared about in bewilderment.

'Where do we start looking, sir?' she asked.

'Well, the fishermen must have been in line with Wrecker's Cove. They said the shapes were coming up on the cliff beyond that - must have been over there.'

Weatherby pointed into the distance. 'We'll have to walk, there's no way the car can get round that rubble.'

Perkins locked the vehicle and followed Weatherby as he bounced from one loose rock to another.

'Might have been easier to leave the car at Smuggler's Halt and walked, sir?' she suggested after ricking her ankle for the second time.

'We don't want to attract anyone's attention and start rumours,' lied Weatherby, who preferred to keep the sea at a safe distance. 'There must be enough of them circulating as it is.'

'Yes, of course. How are we going to tell which of these holes was made by whatever they saw?'

'They measure approximately...' Weatherby took out his notebook, 'Two and a half feet in diameter and one and a half feet deep. I don't know what that is in metric.'

'Well, they probably weren't French anyway,' giggled Perkins.

For a split second Weatherby wished she could meet one.

Managing to cope with the terrain by springing like a small antelope from one rock to another, despite the regulation skirt, Perkins easily overtook the less enthusiastic Weatherby.

He yelled after her, 'Hey! Do you want to encourage these things or something?'

'Well, we don't know what they are, do we, sir?' was the breezy reply.

'They are colossal, short-sighted, and would probably find a young pink WPC very tasty.' Weatherby was convinced she thought it was all a game he had invented for the quiet season.

'Something just moved over there, sir.' Perkins pointed to where the cliff sloped down to the beach.

'Probably rabbits.'

'They must have a tough time burrowing through

this stuff.' She laughed and pranced on her way.

It wasn't until they were well past the spot that the remark struck Weatherby as being quite a logical one for her. The topsoil wasn't deep enough for overweight worms let alone rabbits. Like the good detective he was, he made a mental note to give the spot a wide berth on the way back.

'Found anything. Perkins?' he eventually called to the sickeningly keen constable, hoping her enthusiasm was making her miss the obvious.

But this wasn't going to be his lucky day, 'Over there, sir, I'm sure something moved just below the surface!' She bounded after it, only needing a butterfly net to complete the incongruous picture.

'Come back!' Weatherby yelled with as much force as he could, but she was already jabbing at the spot in the rubble with her baton.

'I think it's all right, sir,' she called as Weatherby desperately tried to reach her over the unsafe ground. 'The rocks here have just been loosened by something.'

'Look, Perkins, don't argue or say anything - just carefully back off, and away from me.'

She turned to look at him in amazement.

'Back off girl, back off!'

Before Perkins was able to make a move, there was a minor eruption. The ground lifted and sandstone cracked like toffee. Rocks flew in every direction, showering Perkins as she stood rooted to the spot.

'Run girl, run!' shouted Weatherby.

Before she could follow his orders, a tentacle threshed through the air and sent her spinning into the track of the monster's massive feet.

Unable to think of anything more effective than hitting the creature with a rock, Weatherby hastily selected the heaviest he could find and hurled it at the evil slit-eyed head. That distracted it long enough for Perkins to find her presence of mind and leap out of its path. She called into her radio for backup, powerless as the mountain of slime and tentacles turned its none too delicate attention to Weatherby.

'Run sir!' she screamed. 'It'll never catch you if you run!'

She wasn't aware of the signal holding Weatherby's mind like a magnet. When he lifted his hands to clutch his head, she thought he had been injured. With the heroism of foolish infatuation, she ran after the towering monster and lashed out as hard as she could with her baton at whatever part presented itself.

Above the noise of their panicking, Perkins heard voices coming up the coast path. A small crowd of people was rushing to their assistance. As she turned back, another of the creatures was standing directly behind her.

'Why don't you run?' she shouted at Weatherby in rage and fright.

The answer was obvious. One of the creature's tentacles had gripped him tightly around the body and he was having enough trouble staying conscious. All he wanted Perkins to do was get away so he could use what was left of his power units. His wish was answered from the most unlikely source. The other creature swished its tentacles through the air and, in its haste to get to Weatherby, hurled Perkins away from the mêlée. She was too stunned to see Weatherby send a jolt of energy through both of the creatures just as they thought they had him securely.

He was lucky that time. There was just enough power left to make them release their hold.

By the time the rescue party had stumbled over the rough ground to them, the robots were lumbering off to disappear into a tunnel they had blasted through the rock. Nobody offered to follow.

Now the cat was out of the bag. Every available

able-bodied person from Smuggler's Halt had run up the cliff path when the coastguard, who had been watching everything through his binoculars, raised the alarm.

Minutes later the place was alive with police cars, a helicopter, and even the coastguard's launch.

Weatherby and Perkins were escorted away with the reverence good clues deserve, and treated for cuts, bruises and shock by the district nurse and a paramedic. Weatherby wouldn't go to hospital, so Perkins refused to as well.

'You stupid woman,' Weatherby scolded when they no longer had an audience. 'Why didn't you run when I told you?'

'And you are a stupid man - sir,' she countered, without so much as an insubordinate blush on her bruised face. 'Why didn't *you* run when I said?'

'I had something on my mind. What's your reason?'

'I was scared stiff. And from where I was it looked as though you were as well.'

Weatherby dipped his head in embarrassment and grinned. Then he started to laugh. He wasn't quite sure why.

***

'Well, now,' Helto observed wryly as she watched the monitor relaying the signal from the robots. 'That was a good way of not attracting too much attention.'

The irony was lost on Insac. 'We'll catch it next time.'

'The Watchers will learn about this before then. You can't perform manoeuvres like that on a backward planet and not expect to be noticed.'

'Now we've fixed the signal, it won't happen again.'

'You're enjoying this, aren't you?'

'No, I'm not, but I'll take over when the time comes if you want.'

'No. I'll do it.'

Insac looked puzzled.

'I think it's self-aware. Its responses indicate a degree of bio-reaction. You might injure it.'

'All right. You'll be impossible to work with afterwards though.'

'That I promise,' Helto warned, 'and I want clearance to transmit a deep space signal.'

'Why? - No, don't tell me. I don't want to know. I'll give you the transmitter key.'

Insac was right. He really wouldn't have wanted to know whom she was going to contact.

***

Three nights later, Weatherby had steeled himself to tell Penny he would be going for good. He had deliberately stayed away for fear of laying his explanation open to prolonged scrutiny. It was evening, but still light. Before calling, he wanted to be sure Paula was in bed and her scandal antennae wouldn't be activated.

Penny opened the door immediately as though she had been waiting for him. He wouldn't accept her invitation to go into the living room and stood with her in the hall.

Weatherby smiled weakly. 'I can't stop, Penny, but had to see you before...' He couldn't bring himself to say any more. The words just ran out.

'You're going after those creatures again, aren't you?' she accused with surprising hardness.

He nodded, not able to tell her it was they who would be chasing him. 'They think the night air is more likely to bring them out.'

'Why didn't you tell me what happened the other day? Don't you trust me?'

Weatherby was confused by her intolerant attitude. 'I didn't want to worry you.'

'It would have worried me a lot less if you'd said something, instead of me having to hear it from gossip in the village.'

'Don't be angry. I'm trying to make it easy as I can.'

'Easy!' Penny nearly shouted, trying to keep her voice down. 'You stand there telling me you might not be coming back because you're going out to get killed by some filthy, slimy, monster, and expect me to accept it as though it was some normal hazard of life? Not even the police can make demands like that! This is what you meant when you told me you'd have to go away the other day, isn't it? At least I should be glad you've actually decided to tell me the truth.'

'But I don't want to be killed by some filthy, slimy monster, Penny,' Weatherby protested. 'You're jumping to conclusions.'

'There's a fair chance of it happening, though? I suppose, as these things took a fancy to you the first time, they reckon they'll come back for a second helping? The army should be dealing with this, not a civilian.'

'Other civilians could be killed if they aren't dealt with. Would you move away from here if I asked?'

'If you came with me.'

Weatherby was so choked he couldn't argue with her, and only just managed, 'Please Penny... I don't want leave you, but if I'm not back by tomorrow morning then you'll know I'm dead. You won't have to go on thinking I'm alive somewhere and hoping I'll return. I wouldn't want you to spend your life wondering where I was.' He found a smile.

Her attitude softened.

'I know Weatherby. I'm being unreasonable. I understand there's always a risk in what you do, but when I saw those army trucks down the road... I don't want to lose you either.' Penny hugged him. 'I'll be here in the morning. Let me know you're all right as soon as you can, won't you?'

'I promised to see Gabrielle before I left,' he whispered in her ear. 'I'll let you break my ribs tomorrow.'

'All right.' As Penny released him she remembered something. 'I want you to drop this in to her if you would.' She picked up a library book from the hall table. 'Then I can stay in all day waiting for you instead of delivering it myself.'

'Silly woman.' Weatherby took the book and kissed her lightly on the lips. 'Say goodnight to Paula for me.'

'Oh, she probably heard every word.'

Before Penny could say any more, he had gone.

CHAPTER 21

As Weatherby stepped from his car, he looked at the sun setting behind the cliff and saw Gabrielle silhouetted against the sky.

'Don't let that watching from the top of the cliff develop into a habit,' he called out cheerfully. 'You know what happened to poor Mr Wendle.' She didn't reply. 'I volunteered to act as monster bait for the army.'

Gabrielle slowly came down and looked at him with a hypnotic, demanding gaze.

'Penny sent this over.' Weatherby handed her the library book. 'The power units have been absorbed,' he added as a matter of fact.

Her expression didn't flicker.

'Tell me, Weatherby,' Gabrielle suddenly asked. 'Have you ever experienced hate?'

Weatherby looked at her in surprise. He thought carefully. 'No - not from my direction anyway.'

'You know what is going to happen to you, yet still don't hate anyone for it?'

'I don't like Penny's first husband too much. He's most likely crazy, so he doesn't count. Why?'

'I just wanted to be sure of something.'

'I sometimes don't think you're quite human either.'

'I sometimes get the same feeling.'

'I reckon all this turmoil over the last few of weeks has had an effect on you.'

'Right again. Thanks for bringing the book. Goodbye, Weatherby.' Without another word Gabrielle went inside the bungalow, leaving him to wonder about the virtues of being human after all.

He reluctantly drove off to his date with monsters from the deep.

All Weatherby needed on top of his fraught encounters with Penny and Gabrielle was an unfriendly Major Clarke Johnson standing at the control point on top of the cliffs giving his opinions to the Captain of the army unit. He could register the man's dislike of him by the swift intake of breath as he approached.

'Taking your time, aren't you, Weatherby,' he snapped.

Oh my god, thought Weatherby, the man used my name. It had to be either a bizarre form of respect, or abuse, so he replied sweetly, 'I'm sure they're not going to run away as soon as they know I've arrived. Nice clear night for a bloody battle,' he added, to make sure everyone knew his opinion of professional fighters.

The Captain was unsure what to make of the detective in the fancy waistcoat. 'Yes, well... Let's hope it doesn't come to that. How much do you think one of these landed leviathans weighs?'

'Too much,' muttered Weatherby under his breath, and then saw that the Captain was waiting for a reply. 'Several tons, I should think.'

'Can't be more specific can you, sir? We may need

to use heavy artillery. Whatever they are, I only hope they're not some protected species the conservationists are liable to have our guts over.'

'Oh, no whale could be as stroppy as this pair.'

'They must have been three and a half tons each at least,' a voice piped up from the milling blue uniforms. Perkins's bruised face appeared, smiling from the throng as though she was on a picnic.

'Thank you, miss.' The Captain sighed, obviously thinking them both mad. 'We'd better set the artillery up over there!' He shouted to his sergeant then went off to supervise the operation.

'What are you doing here, Perkins?' demanded Weatherby in annoyance.

'Why not, sir? Everybody else is, whether they're on duty or not.'

'You don't imagine for one moment that you're going out there to act as bait as well, do you?'

'Well of course, isn't that what you're going to do?'

'Oh no you're not.'

'Why not, sir?'

'Because pink obviously isn't their colour. They prefer the taste of ageing black detective. Now get back to the control unit before I handcuff you to a lamp post.'

'Aren't any about here, sir.' Perkins, seeing a look of thunder pass over Weatherby's usually amiable features, backed away. 'All right, sir. If you insist.'

'You can look after this for me.' He took off his jacket and handed it to her. His satin waistcoat shone like a paisley beacon. 'Just in case I have to run.'

'You will this time, sir?'

'Promise,' lied Weatherby with a smile, and waved her away.

Major Clarke Johnson had watched their little discussion with stern disapproval. Weatherby would have liked to tell him what in fact was going to happen, just to see his reaction, but the Captain was calling to him from the higher ground where the gun was being erected. Beaming the Major a quick insincere smile, Weatherby made his way towards it.

The Captain was calculating his strategy. 'I think you should walk in a semicircle from the lower path to see how our lights pick you out to begin with. Don't get too near the beach. It's just a dummy run.'

'Fine,' agreed Weatherby. 'How will these creatures know it's a trial run?'

'Don't go too far, and there's still some light. I'll be sending armed men with you when you go round the next time.' The Captain obviously wanted to catch one whole to give his troops a challenge and MOD scientists something to play with. 'Don't worry, sir, my men are crack marksmen.'

'Thanks. I promise to look after them.'

'It was one of the conditions of letting you do this, Weatherby,' said a stern voice, the only one to genuinely make him apprehensive. Weatherby turned and saw his Commissioner. 'As soon as these creatures appear, you are to get out of there and leave everything to the army. D'you understand?'

Weatherby could feel his body standing to attention against his will. 'Yes, sir.'

'And don't go and fall down some pothole like a ruddy fool. Good luck.' Before Weatherby could think of a reply, he was gone.

The detective marvelled at the attention he was receiving prior to doing his brave deed, and wondered what splendid niceties would be lavished on his mortal remains - if they were ever found reasonably near each other. He tried to entertain himself with the thought that androids couldn't feel pain - it didn't work.

When he was isolated in the limpid illumination of the distant searchlights, and too far from the heavy artillery for comfort, he realised all too well he was no longer a mechanoid. Pain was part of the mortality package he had opted for, along with heartache, angst, anger and no two-year guarantee.

His knees started to buckle and he was relieved to get back to the footpath again. The cool night breeze blew the telltale perspiration from his body before he reached the Captain.

'Splendid, splendid,' the soldier said, having lined him up in his men's gunsights as well as the searchlights. 'Nothing would stand a chance from here.'

Weatherby became momentarily distracted by the hopeful prospect of a quick death. 'Including me,' he muttered.

The Captain coughed to attract Weatherby's attention. 'We're ready to go now, sir. You can make the circle a bit wider. I'll have four men follow directly after you.'

'Right.' Weatherby started out once more over the treacherous landscape.

As the reality of the situation began to hit home, he wished there were no soldiers to see him going into meltdown. They obviously weren't expecting some slimy, monstrous thing to rise from the depths of solid rock.

Not so much as a flaw appeared in the rocky ground and Weatherby felt more reassured. By the time they were on their third circuit, he felt bold enough to lead them further out.

'Better keep in range of the gun, sir,' warned the corporal. 'We don't know how effective these rifles would be if we meet one of these things.' His tone suggested that he was bored with the whole business and the appearance of a monster or two would be a welcome relief.

Weatherby straightened his path towards the ground that was easier to negotiate, and he made his way unsuspectingly to the perimeter of the searchlight. Had the beam reached further, it would have picked out the grotesque mound waiting to make its clumsy pounce.

No signal tugged at his brain, so he assumed it was safe enough. As an ex android he should have realised it was a mistake to underestimate the minds that had programmed both of them. Perhaps he was going to live long enough to comprehend the deviousness of his creators and that this reality didn't fight fair after all.

Then, on the other hand...

A robot's tentacles lashed out from nowhere and seized Weatherby. He let out a startled yelp. In the same instant the soldiers were in position, firing at the creature's head as the heavy artillery had to sit idly by while Weatherby tried to struggle free. Another searchlight picked out the robot's companion, lumbering towards the party. The gun crew trained their sights on it before it got too close to the other one. With a report that shook the watching Smuggler's Halt, a shell smashed into its target. When the smoke cleared it was apparent that the creature had actually managed to quicken its pace. The Captain went several shades of red, white and blue in rage, terror, and shock, as he realised he was going to be the unfortunate to have to explain this in a report.

'Fire again before it gets any closer!' he ordered, with more than a tinge of desperation. The blast drowned his next order to the assembled troops to charge over the terrain.

He was too late. The monsters had escaped down their tunnel with Weatherby and sealed its entrance. By the time the smoke cleared and the soldiers had reached the spot, all trace of them was gone. The four soldiers were in a state of shock and too blinded by smoke to tell which way they went. Some vainly tried

to pick out their elephantine tracks, but the ground
was too pitted to identify them in the harsh glare of
the searchlight.

After the Police Commissioner had made his
thorough way over the scene of the crime, his
personnel could find nothing but the fob watch
Weatherby had worn ever since his metal watch strap
had burned an old man's hand.

There was nothing they could do at that moment.

'We'll have to start a search in the morning.'

As the Commissioner, flanked by several of his
officers, made his impressive progress through the
silent gathering, Dot whispered into Gabrielle's ear,
'Don't think we should say anything to your Aunt
Penny about this, should we, dear?'

'We can't be too sure what happened from this
distance anyway.' Gabrielle smiled wryly. 'And they
aren't likely to tell us, or the press.'

'No. But I can take a good guess.'

'Poor Weatherby. Penny will never get over this.'

CHAPTER 22

Helto came back on shift and took her place before the
monitor.

'The robots moved it to the nearest station,' Insac
told her. 'I sent them back, but won't cocoon them until
we've finished. The tunnels will have to be serviced.'

Helto thought there was something wrong with
laws that allowed lumbering great monsters like that
on other peoples' planets, yet not inoffensive, albeit
disobedient, androids. 'I suppose they succeeded in
totally disrupting the life of the area before they went?'

'You're the authority on insubordination, so I won't
argue. Now we have it, don't take too long carrying out
the scan. Send the results to the technicians as soon as
you have them. Make sure they are thorough. We may

not get another chance to find out why this unit malfunctioned.' A doubt struck Insac as he was about to leave. 'Are you sure you want to do this?'

'I'll do it. You know you can trust me.'

'Yes, I know.' He left Helto to get on with the job in peace.

She turned her attention to the monitor as soon as he had gone. Weatherby was being held between two pillows of air pressure, ready for the laboratory equipment to operate on him.

'Hello Kybion,' Helto said.

Weatherby was unable to answer because there was a tube in his mouth flushing fluid through his digestive tract. Though not painful, it was undignified. He also didn't welcome a one-sided conversation with the ceiling.

'I'm sorry if you find this unpleasant, but we have to do this before we use the probe. You would insist on developing the sort of anatomy we can't take apart and test. We need you alive to do this.'

Weatherby wondered whether it would have been better for him if the robots had torn him apart or, better still, he had become the victim of friendly fire from the friendly corporal and his men. At least it would have been a glorious death and Penny would have had a posthumous medal to remember him by.

'Don't try to struggle. Nothing I do will hurt you.' As though she could hear Weatherby calling her a liar, Helto added, 'I'll make everything as easy as possible.'

There was something ponderous in her tone that suggested she was going to take as long as she possibly could and probably allow his newly acquired bowels to be washed away completely.

Then Helto removed the pump.

'Thanks...' Weatherby gasped, 'though I'd prefer to be put down before you carry out the autopsy.'

'We need to monitor your body reactions while

they're still functioning. Why not try to relax?'

'Relax? I'm not one of your mindless mechanical mistakes. I'm delicate and don't like being patronised.'

Helto pondered for a moment. 'Your biology is now so human I would like to run a scan to see how successful the transition was.'

'I don't need to be told whether my biology's real or not. I can feel it.'

'Interesting.'

'How are you going to insert the scanning equipment?' he eventually found the courage to ask.

Helto avoided the question. 'Oh, we aren't going to cut you up.'

***

When Gabrielle returned to the bungalow, she made herself a cup of coffee and took it to the settee where she sat with her legs tucked beneath her, thinking. She watched the minutes tick by on the well-polished face of Wendle's old grandfather clock. As the brass hands drew near midnight she let her legs relax into a more comfortable position, and closed her eyes.

Slowly her conscious thoughts moved from her body and she visited the laboratory deep in the Earth's ocean where Weatherby was being held captive. In the next instant, she was light years away, standing at the shoulder of Helto as she impatiently tapped her console, casting anxious glances at a row of unlit signal lights.

'You will not feel anything,' she was telling Weatherby as a fine filament was fed into his mouth.

To Weatherby's surprise she was right.

'I'll do the brain scan now. Keep your thoughts still.'

By the way Helto was playing for time, Gabrielle knew she had to act quickly. Now in command of her Star Dancer nature, she went straight to Ojal. Her subconscious could dawdle and gawp at the wonders of the Universe another time.

An unsuspecting Anaru had just activated her loop. From it, the Star Dancer suddenly demanded, 'Fetch Controller Opu.'

The seer found herself looking straight into the demanding dark eyes of a very serious human being and almost leapt out of the loop in surprise.

'There is no time to explain. Do it now,' ordered Gabrielle.

Anaru dashed into her alcove and sent out the call.

Opu wasn't in the control room or her own home. It was only by pure chance that Anaru found her about to leave Annac's home with her small brat. Noting the urgency in Anaru's garbled message, Opu gave Annac the dubious pleasure of looking after Opuna while she flew off to find out what the problem was.

When Opu joined Anaru in the loop, she was amazed to be confronted by the Star Dancer.

The controller was still fearful of the power the creature possessed. 'What do you want?'

'You received a message from Taigal Rax. It was about the android you sent to Earth.'

Opu was fazed for a minute. This wasn't the blazing, devouring entity she recognised. Its thoughts were calm, controlled... And very, very ominous.

'You mean Perimeter 84926? Yes. It was malfunctioning, so they're going to dismantle it. What's wrong?' she compelled herself to reply.

'You agree with their actions?'

'Of course. It would have been against the law to let it wander about on that planet. We don't want any trouble. We've had all we need for a long while.' Opu hoped that hadn't sounded like an accusation. This entity could still beat the planet up, if not totally annihilate it.

The Star Dancer had other things on her mind.

'You must contact Taigal Rax and tell them to stop this.'

Why was it always down to her to do the impossible? 'I can't,' protested Opu. 'I don't like the idea of breaking up something that sophisticated, but there's no way we can get it back to Taigal Rax.'

'You must leave it where it is.'

However threatening this Star Dancer, that was a demand too far. Opu hadn't saved Ojal just to have it disintegrated. 'That would bring the collected wrath of the Watchers down on us, human! Don't you understand that the price of evolution is self-control?'

'The law has already been broken by the robots sent after it. Stop the procedure now.'

'Why all this over one android?'

'I will tell you why,' Gabrielle said.

***

There had been nothing unpleasant about the brain scan, apart from a barrage of sound waves that made Weatherby's skull vibrate a little, and a more relaxed position helped to ease his dismayed digestive tract. He even found himself becoming interested in what Helto was doing.

'Why are you taking so long over this?'

'Would you rather I rushed things?' Helto hoped he wasn't in too much of a hurry to be dismantled.

'No. As long as you keep it painless, I'm happy to go on living for as long as you like.'

He could hear a voice in the background asking Helto, 'Is that all you've done?'

'You said everything had to be thorough.'

'Well, it doesn't matter to me,' Insac's voice echoed clearly from the ceiling. 'It will make a lot of difference to the android if it's as sophisticated as those brain scans show. Do you want me to take over?'

'No,' Weatherby could hear Helto faintly scold.

'Just go away.'

Weatherby wasn't sure whether to panic right away, or wait until he knew what was going to happen. The fact that Helto didn't speak to him for a painful length of time wasn't reassuring.

'We have to go on to the body scan now,' her voice announced without warning.

Weatherby had quite forgotten the filament threaded throughout his body. 'What's going to happen?' Though he preferred to die of surprise before he found out.

'Will you trust me?' Helto asked.

'If you're going to dismantle me at any moment, that seems somewhat irrelevant.'

'I meant, could you believe I am trying to help you?'

'No,' said Weatherby. 'Why should I?'

'I can't tell you.'

Weatherby felt an odd crawling sensation in his stomach. It was hardly butterflies

'What is that?' he demanded.

'The body scan.'

As the crawling sensation spread throughout his body he felt as though every organ was being poked and squeezed.

'I prefer pain!' he blurted out.

'It's only caused by the scan cord sending out impulses to examine your organs.'

'I don't care,' Weatherby protested. 'I don't like it.' The bruising sensations intensified and Weatherby could see the scan cord glowing inside his body. 'Turn it off!'

'Don't panic. When it's finished the cord will dissolve.'

Helto switched off her a transmitter and began collating the incoming data. She shot an occasional glance at the line of signal lights. None of them so much as flickered. Helto wished she was callous enough to prolong the body scan. She weakened and let the scan run down, then sat looking blankly at the semiconscious Weatherby.

Insac returned and saw Helto gazing vacantly at the monitor.

'You've got to finish now. It's pointless leaving it in that condition.'

'I know.' With one last look towards the signal lights on the console, Helto activated the beam that would dismember Weatherby's body.

'I can't stand this,' Insac muttered to himself as the reality of what they were doing occurred to him.

'It's better to do it before he recovers,' Helto said. 'Do you still want to take over?'

'No thanks, I'm beginning to feel a bit strange about it as well.'

'What for? This is our job. To maintain and control robots and androids we have planted on other planets, and then break them up when they don't do as they are told.'

Insac read the completed data. 'Look at these results! They actually did it! They made an android that turned into a living being. There was nothing wrong with it after all.'

'Well, let's hope there's a law passed soon, so we don't have to go through all this again.' Helto lined up the beam. 'I'll remove the head first. It's the best way.'

CHAPTER 23

Perkins spent all night trying to keep out of everyone's way as she carried on searching for her colleague. The young constable been ordered off duty for rest and recuperation after the battering she had received from the marauding monsters, so few people paid attention to her presence in the confusion of the night before.

About six o'clock in the morning there were only
three policemen patrolling the beach, waiting for the
search party to arrive. Perkins was exhausted by that
time. She wanted to rest, yet couldn't bring herself to
go home while Weatherby was still missing. Then she
remembered Gabrielle. Her bungalow was easy to find,
and she gingerly knocked on the door. To her surprise,
a girl her own age opened it right away. She was fully
dressed and looked as though she had been wide
awake for hours.

'I hope you don't mind me calling on you at this
time in the morning..?' She began. 'I'm Perkins.'

Gabrielle smiled. 'Of course. Weatherby's told me
all about you.'

The young woman's face fell. 'Really?'

'Only the good bits... and the one about the
parakeet on the chimney.'

'Well, I didn't know that they bred in the wild.'

'Didn't believe a word of it. He probably removed
the ladder himself. That man's got a strange sense of
humour. You look as though you've been up all night.'
Gabrielle waved Perkins inside.

'I've been looking for Mr Weatherby. I daren't let
anyone else see me, or I'll be ordered to go home.'

'Well - if you will go about attacking slimy
monsters from the deep.' Gabrielle poured her a cup of
red bush tea. 'Why not drink this and get a couple of
hours sleep?'

'I don't think I could. I can't stop thinking about
what happened to Mr Weatherby.'

'Oh he's all right. He's grown his own self-
preservation circuit.'

Perkins burst into tears.

'He was such a lovely man,' she blubbered until
Gabrielle handed her a tissue. 'You should have seen
what happened up there... it was terrible.'

'Look, why don't you have a nap, then we'll go and

search along the beach together?'

'All right,' Perkins agreed.

'I'll wake you up in a couple of hours,' Gabrielle promised. 'You'll feel a lot better then.' She hesitated. 'Why "Mr" Weatherby, not Guv?'

The young woman had to think. 'I couldn't call him Guv, it would be disrespectful.'

Gabriel wondered what Perkins' colleagues made of her but, when she thought about it, the man probably did deserve some respect.

***

Controller Opu dashed through the air like a thing possessed towards the control of Main Base Station 93. Other Ojalies had learnt to get out of her flight path, and she fell to the floor of the balcony without having caused any mid-air disasters. Opu pounced on the console, much to the surprise of the controller operating it.

As she tried to open transmission to Taigal Rax, the operator said, 'Didn't you know that the link was severed shortly after the last transmission? Something to do with gravitational interference.'

Opu didn't say a word. She swayed giddily, then dashed back to the balcony where she leapt into the air again, only bothering to open her wings after she was airborne.

'What was all that about?' asked the startled controller.

'No idea,' another replied. 'But you know what she's been like since the emergency. And having to cope with that brat of hers can't help.'

Annac, whose curiosity had got the better of her, had arrived to see Anaru. She had just made Opuna secure in her light cubicle when Opu piled up on the small balcony behind the light beam curtain.

'The link's been severed,' she gasped.

'Gravitational interference. Get Healphani on the loop quick.'

'I can't do that,' Anaru protested. 'It's nothing like the correct transmission time.'

'If we can't stop them dismembering that android, we'll have more trouble than a dozen Star Dancers.'

Annac had no idea what was going on. 'Why?'

'No time to explain. Please try, Anaru. You must know what will happen if we can't reach them.'

'From the way Healphani spoke, it's probably too late.' The seer read total annihilation in Opu's eyes. 'All right, but I'm afraid that android will be spare parts by the time I make contact.' She switched on the power.

'Android?' demanded Annac. 'Why all this bother about an android?'

'Because the Kybion isn't an android any more,' Opu admitted.

'You mean the one you used the Kybini System to transmit to Perimeter 84926 actually developed into a living thing?' She chortled in delight. 'That's marvellous.'

Opu was amazed at her reaction. Senility must have been making Annac lose perspective. 'It's not if you're the android at the moment, or Ojal if we can't stop it from being broken up.'

'What's the problem? You sound as though the Star Dancer is threatening to come back?' Opu was suspiciously quiet, so Annac insisted, 'If it started out as an android, then it can't be registered as anything else.'

'There is no known precedent. Androids can be dismantled. Living creatures can't.'

A glimmer of understanding registered in Annac's face. 'Ah. I knew those robot engineers would get too clever for their own good one day.'

'Shut up, you two, I'm trying to concentrate.'

Anaru transmitted her thoughts at Taigal Rax with every ounce of skill she had. 'It's no good. They're just not expecting us at the moment.'

'Try scanning the planet,' Opu told her. 'Get hold of anyone.'

'Only someone like Healphani would be believed carrying a message like that.'

'I'll give the code to the first person you contact.'

Annac and Anaru stared at Opu in amazement.

'It's the only way.'

At any other time it would have been gratifying to see the alarm on Annac's face.

'You mean it was *her?*'

Even Opuna stopped trying to escape from the light cubicle on the other side of the room and started to watch intently.

Annac swallowed hard. 'That's not possible.'

'Oh yes it is. If this message doesn't get through, we'll all end up as star dust,' Opu told her.

'And I always thought that android was incompetent.'

'It wasn't. Apparently it was too efficient.'

They sat watching Anaru's screen in silence. Nothing happened for a painfully long while.

Annac whispered to Opu, 'Surely the Star Dancer could have gone straight to Taigal Rax?'

'The warning originated from Taigal Rax, but from an illegal source that couldn't pass on the code. It has to be delivered by an untainted carrier, and the Star Dancer's manifestation wouldn't be recognised.'

'This is going to take forever.'

Eventually something shuddered onto the screen.

Annac joined the loop. 'What is that?'

A wide-skulled, black-scaled creature was peering back at them in surprise. It blinked in disbelief once or twice, and then some of its babbling thoughts spluttered into the loop. 'I knew I should stop diving to these depths. Now I'm beginning to hallucinate.'

'Can you see us?' Anaru demanded with such authority the diver replied despite himself.

'I can see and hear something inside my head.'

'That's me talking to you. There is nothing wrong with you. You are not hallucinating. You are a sensitive.'

'Who, me?' the diver was incredulous. 'I'm only maintenance. And I'm only that because I'm not bright enough to be anything else. Me a sensitive? Never.'

'If that's all the use you are,' interrupted Opu, 'then it won't be beneath you to deliver a message for us to your nearest control station.'

The black-scaled diver became suspicious. 'You're not playing a trick on me, are you? Don't you surface breathers never have anything better to do.'

'What do we have to say to convince you that you are a sensitive who has it in his power to save someone's life?'

'Oh...'

'This message has to be delivered by a sensitive. It wouldn't be accepted from a non sensitive surface breather.'

The diver was convinced. Surface breathers never mocked themselves. 'What do you want me to do?'

'You must remember a symbol, and a simple message. You have to concentrate very deeply while we put the symbol into your mind.'

'Oh, I'm no good at remembering things.'

'You must try.'

'I'm so useless at remembering things I have to carry a sequence board or I forget what I'm supposed to be doing. I daren't go anywhere without it.'

Opu was in a near frenzy. 'Well, draw the symbol on that!'

'Keep calm, keep calm. You can't rush this fellow,' Anaru had to remind her.

The diver lifted his board and held a writing instrument over it in readiness. 'All right.'

Anaru and Opu jointly drew the symbol in their minds and the diver laboriously copied it onto the board.

'Now write this beneath it,' Opu told him. 'Ready?'

'Ready.'

'The Kybion... must... not... be... dismantled. Opu.'

Not knowing he was being transmitted the words by somebody with a completely alien tongue, the diver automatically wrote it down in his own language; Opu couldn't tell if he had it right or wrong.

'Is that all?' the bewildered diver asked.

'Yes. Remember, if you don't hurry to the nearest station and hand that message over, someone will die.'

'All right.' Having decided to believe that the conversation inside his head had been real, the diver swam off in such a leisurely way, the other three wondered whether his good intentions were going to be enough.

'He'll never make it in time, wherever the nearest station is.' Opu buried her beak in her hands.

'Oh, don't worry,' Annac told her. 'By the shape of his body and colouring, he must have been at quite a depth. He'll move faster as he ascends.'

'I hope you're right... I just hope you're right.' Opu turned in time to see her brat scrambling out of the light cubicle and advancing towards her. 'Now what do you want?' she asked irritably. The child affectionately sank its beak into her arm. 'I suppose that serves me right for asking,' Opu rubbed the wound. 'I'm sure she's a throwback.'

***

Weatherby didn't try to struggle when he saw the cutting beam hover over his head. As it snaked down towards his neck, he closed his eyes and hoped the end would be quick. All the time he could hear Insac and Helto talking.

'Use more power. It'll make a cleaner incision.'

Weatherby could feel the heat of the beam as Helto did as Insac said.

'He's so tense, it's impossible to be accurate. Are you sure there isn't any way to stun him?'

'No. Androids have never needed anaesthetics before.'

Weatherby felt the beam on his neck and tried to faint.

Then he heard Helto calling, 'Quick, answer that!'

'All right.' After a brief pause, Insac snapped, 'Cut that thing out quick!'

He obviously wasn't referring to Weatherby's neck. The beam immediately disappeared.

'This is a countermand from Central,' lnsac accused.

'Well I never,' said Helto. 'I wonder why they've done that?'

'And there's a code symbol. Who did you contact when I gave you the transmitter key?' There was a pause as Insac checked the console. 'There's been interdimensional traffic on here.'

'Yes,' agreed Helto. 'Isn't technology wonderful?'

CHAPTER 24

Gabrielle stood for some time on top of the cliff, scouring every inch of sea and beach lit by the early morning sun. Eventually she saw what she was looking for and went back to the bungalow to rouse Perkins. Still only half awake, and without bothering to put on her tie, jacket or hat, or tuck in her shirt, she dashed after Gabrielle, down the path to the pebble beach.

Gabrielle pointed to a crumpled heap lying at the

water's edge. Perkins was unable to fathom what it was as the sun's rays glistened on the wet bundle. It looked like a body. Her police officer's instincts kicked in and she ran to investigate.

The nearer she got, the more familiar it became, until the waistcoat was unmistakable.

'Mr Weatherby! Mr Weatherby! Are you all right?' she called.

Perkins hauled him into a sitting position without first bothering to find out whether he was conscious.

Weatherby's eyes suddenly opened wide in amazement as he saw his subordinate and felt her fingers sink into his tender flesh.

'Say something, sir! Say something!' she demanded.

He winced at her none too delicate attention. 'Perkins, you are improperly dressed.'

As there was nothing unusual in the remark, she took it to mean that he was feeling as well as could be expected.

Gabrielle reached them. 'Haven't you anything else to say to us?'

Weatherby thought in wide-eyed confusion for a moment, unable to work out how he had arrived there and why his body throbbed so much that even the pressure of his buttoned waistcoat was painful.

'I can't think of anything. Only, undo my waistcoat one of you.' Perkins immediately obliged with her usual enthusiasm. 'Carefully!'

'There's something wrong with him,' Gabrielle warned. 'We'll have to call some paramedics. He can't move in that condition.'

Perkins went to pull out her mobile, only to find that she wasn't wearing a jacket because she was improperly dressed.

'Don't you dare!' snapped Weatherby.

'Well, whatever it is, it hasn't made him any less

obstreperous,' observed Gabrielle.

'I'll walk.'

Perkins looked back at the steep path. 'Up there? In your condition?'

'Stop arguing woman. I'll do it.'

Gabrielle seized his arm. 'There's no point in reasoning with the man. You won't get any promotion for trying. Help me get him up. We'll see if he can walk to the bungalow.'

Somehow the young women managed to struggle up the cliff path with him. Once at the top, Weatherby shook them off. Perkins still wanted to call for an ambulance, but he was adamant. He even refused to let her notify anyone he'd been found and made the rest of his way to the bungalow unaided.

When they reached the living room, Gabrielle told Weatherby in a no-nonsense way, 'We have to tell the others to call the search off. Perkins can take your car and pick up a change of clothes for you.'

Weatherby sat on the settee, too exhausted to argue.

'You'll see a doctor as well.'

'No!' Weatherby insisted. 'I don't want any doctor near me.'

'He's just being irrational,' Gabrielle told Perkins. 'Do you feel up to doing all that?'

'Oh yes, I've got his jacket with the keys,' she agreed brightly, her old scatterbrained self again at finding her lost head boy, even though his manners hadn't improved.

She quickly pulled on the rest of her uniform and sped off.

'I don't want to see anyone,' Weatherby complained.

'I know,' agreed Gabrielle, 'but the effects won't last forever.'

Weatherby looked at her uncertainly. 'You know

what happened?'

'Yes.'

'Then it must have been you who stopped them?'

'Maybe.'

'You threatened Ojal with the Star Dancer again, didn't you? All hell will break loose if you've done that! You'll have committed a crime against Galactic Law!'

'Nothing dreadful is going to happen.'

'You don't know what you've done. You should have left me.'

'It's all right.' Gabrielle dried his head and neck. 'I'll explain it all to you as a wedding present.' She looked at the algae staining the towel. 'You need a shower.'

'I thought you were glad to see me go?'

'Perhaps I've grown fond of you in a funny sort of way.'

'You've a funny way of showing it.'

'You had access to more data in a galactic library and all you could use it for was to become romantic. Someone like you deserves to be understood.'

Weatherby could only think about the Watcher who was bound to catch up with them sooner or later. 'So what happens now?'

'You'd better get cleaned up. Half the county's police force and umpteen soldiers will probably turn up on the doorstep at any minute and want you to pose for pictures.'

'You're mad. You haven't a clue what you've done, have you?' He resentfully picked up the phone, only to have second thoughts and replace the receiver. 'I'll make the call a when I've had a shower and Perkins brings some clothes.'

'Better be quick. She's already told everyone.'

'What? Perkins? I told her not to.'

A siren could be heard in the distance.

'You really haven't got the hang of humans yet,

have you?'

'Don't open the door!'

'Ten second shower then.'

Gabrielle found a dressing gown of Wendle's for Weatherby to slip on. Though Wendle had been much smaller, it sufficed until his own clothes turned up via a breathless Perkins. She had been the one sounding the siren. The young policewoman had also notified HQ, but supplied misleading directions to give Weatherby time to make himself presentable before they arrived. It didn't work. Smuggler's Halt was thronged with uniforms before he could step out of the shower.

To make matters worse, the Commissioner turned up in time to see him in a ridiculously small dressing gown, and demand to know what had happened. Weatherby was unable to think of any plausible story, insisting he had lost consciousness when the creatures carried him off, and only remembered waking up on the beach. This was unexplained phenomena territory and the explanation was gratefully accepted. The Commissioner promised him a commendation and medal as insurance against Weatherby suddenly remembering and writing a book about the experience.

When the news leaked out, Smuggler's Halt had the occasional influx of psychics and UFO spotters. The number of holidaymakers didn't increase, and that stretch of shore became peculiarly deserted for months. For some reason people weren't anxious to meet slimy, lumbering monsters and shake one of their many tentacles.

Apart from the brief phone call Gabrielle made that morning to tell her that Weatherby was safe, Penny knew nothing of what had gone on. This didn't bother her too much because she was very good at guessing. All she wanted to do when she saw him standing at the front door in his shirtsleeves was to

deliver the long hard hug she had started to give him
the night before. Despite the pain, Weatherby said
nothing. Then Penny realised that something was
wrong.

'Why aren't you wearing your waistcoat,
Weatherby?' she released him. 'You always wear a
waistcoat?'

'I'm putting on weight,' he lied. 'I had trouble doing
the buttons up. Why do you only want to hug me when
I've got a waistcoat on?' He tried to embrace her.

She backed away, fixing him with a suspicious
look. 'Come inside, Weatherby.'

He did as he was told, getting used to Penny's
sudden changes of mood. She herded him into the
living room and closed the door behind her.

'Now what?' he asked, unsure how to react.

'We aren't teenage sweethearts, Weatherby. We're
adults. If neither of us can trust the other to tell them
things that matter, we might as well be strangers. I
don't mind you not wanting to talk about your past life,
or how many lovers you've had, and I know you'd never
he a policeman if you had a record or were mentally
disturbed. And I don't particularly want to talk about
my past, but I do mind you keeping things from me
that matter. I want to know when there's a chance of
you being killed or injured. And I want to know when
you *have* been injured.' Weatherby glanced nervously
at the door. 'It's all right, Paula's playing round at
Angela's, so don't worry about her bursting in.' Penny
paused. 'Do you want us to get married?'

Weatherby wondered how she could have doubted
it. It showed in his expression.

'You should really be in hospital, shouldn't you?'

'I wouldn't like the food.' He couldn't stop himself
sounding emotional. 'And I wouldn't want to make you
travel all that way every time you wanted to scold me.'

'Oh, Weatherby, I wouldn't scold if you trusted me.'

She kissed him as passionately as his delicate condition would allow.

'When?' asked Weatherby when he thought it was safe to.

'When what?'

'When are we going to be married? You are sure you want marry me, aren't you, Penny?'

'Looks as though I'll have to now I'm going to make you take your shirt off. Let's wait until Jack and Connie can get down, then they can stop with Gabrielle.'

'Paula won't mind us getting married?' Weatherby asked unsurely.

'Of course she won't. When we have our honeymoon she can stop with Gabrielle as well.'

'Gabrielle might not appreciate all that company,' Weatherby warned her.

'Of course she won't mind for a couple of weeks. I don't know why you two are so funny about each other.'

'We're probably kindred spirits in a way.'

'How do you mean?' asked Penny.

'Oh, she knows what she wants, but won't tell anyone else what it is. I know what I want, and everyone in the Universe knows I've got it.'

Penny laughed and kissed him again.

CHAPTER 25

Later that summer Gabrielle was working part time in the village library before going to university. Her foster parents, Jack and Connie, had arrived at the bungalow the week before the wedding to be held in the town's registry office. They spent most of their time making plans for the reception to follow in the village hotel.

Weatherby had developed the habit of turning up to see Penny every evening, or sending Perkins over to make sure she hadn't run off with someone else. Even

Perkins was going to be relieved when her superior
was safely married. But Paula was getting the best out
of the situation; a new dress, regular pocket money
from Weatherby, occasional ride in a police car, and
being chief bridesmaid at her mother's wedding.

There was little formality in the service at the
registry office. All concerned, especially Weatherby,
who was expecting to be struck by a thunderbolt at any
moment, was anxious to get it over with. The main
point of interest with the guests was how the
bridegroom had managed to find the astonishing
waistcoat that clashed so well with Penny's brocade
two-piece.

After the dash to the hotel reception and obligatory
speeches, few guests seemed to notice that the couple
they had been toasting were nowhere to be found.
There was no reason why mature lovers should
exercise any more restraint than younger ones, so
nobody tried to look for them: no one except a young
woman with the penetrating gaze of a mystic.
Weatherby and Penny were aware that Gabrielle was
only a short distance away from them in the hotel
garden. She seemed to be watching everything but
what they were doing.

Connie and Jack were delighted that their foster
daughter had become so mature in such a short time,
and was growing into an independent woman.
Gabrielle's rapid development only appeared to be
sinister to Weatherby who was expecting to be dealt
cosmic retribution at any second and, worse still,
Penny finding out the truth about him. It would have
eased his mind a little if the mysterious young woman
showed little more concern. Perhaps some sort of
delusion prevented her from realising the gravity of
their situation.

Penny smiled at Weatherby's preoccupation. 'What
are you thinking about, lover? No beer garden's worth

that much attention.'

'I was just wondering what Gabrielle was looking at.'

'Well, I'm looking at you. Now turn this way and do some wondering about me.'

'She looks like a stone sentinel standing there.'

'I don't know why she worries you so much. It's as though you two share some dreadful secret.'

Weatherby tried not to look dismayed at her accurate observation, and hugged Penny to distract her.

Suddenly an abrasive voice rang out from the adjoining orchard gate.

'I warned you, didn't I, Pen?' barked a thin-featured man in a faded brown suit that matched the colour of his insane, motionless eyes.

'Frank!' screamed Penny, and pulled herself in front of Weatherby.

He had totally forgotten the warnings her first husband had been making. As soon as Weatherby saw the revolver in the man's hand he threw himself in front of Penny. That was just what Frank wanted. Without a word of explanation he aimed at the splendid target of Weatherby's waistcoat and with cool, cruel premeditation squeezed the trigger twice. The reports echoed about the hotel grounds.

Penny was too stunned to scream. She clung onto Weatherby as though he'd be all right if he wasn't allowed to collapse to the ground.

Penny was still holding onto him when his police colleagues dashed out from the reception and leapt on Frank as though he were dessert. He was pinned to the ground and disarmed.

'Weatherby, Weatherby!' Penny called over his shoulder. 'Are you all right?' She daren't turn him round to look at his chest.

Weatherby looked back at her. He sounded

amazed. 'Yes Penny. Nothing hit me. I didn't feel a
thing.'

'He must have missed you,' said Jack, running up
to them, his face glowing with relief and champagne.
'Bullets could have gone anywhere. Just like a copper
to bring his work to his wedding reception. '

'But he fired at point-blank range, Jack,' Penny
insisted. 'He couldn't have missed.'

'If he was sane, perhaps, though I don't reckon he
ever was.'

'I don't know how, but Weatherby's still alive.'

'Perhaps Heaven wasn't ready for me,' Weatherby
smiled to hide the apprehension that had overtaken
his astonishment. Those bullets hadn't been blanks.
Frank was unbalanced, not incompetent. 'You ever
heard of a black angel?'

'Fool.' Penny recovered her composure. 'I can see
I'll have to knit you a bullet proof vest.'

Jack grinned. 'I thought that waistcoat might have
been bullet proof, myself. 'I can't see any other
explanation for it.'

'I have taste,' Weatherby told his brother-in-law.
'It may be odd taste, but Penny likes it.'

Connie came across the lawn to collect her
husband. 'Come back into the reception and leave
those two alone, Jack. We might as well keep the party
going. There are enough police here to handle Frank.
He'd like nothing more than to know he spoiled the
wedding.'

'And the bridegroom,' Weatherby whispered to
Penny. Over her shoulder, he could see Gabrielle still
standing like a stone sentinel. She had been totally
unmoved by the incident. As a possible explanation for
his deliverance occurred to him, he froze.

Later Penny had to honour a promise she made
some months before, and spend an hour with her office
colleagues at the town hall. Even Weatherby was

excluded from the hen party, but then, he had
something more pressing to deal with.

The guests dispersed. As Paula, Jack, and Connie
walked back to the bungalow, Weatherby followed the
enigmatic Gabrielle to the pebbled beach where she sat
on a breakwater, waiting for him.

He kept his distance and called, 'What happened?'

'I can't shout from here without telling the whole
of Smuggler's Halt. Come closer,' Gabrielle told him.

He reluctantly obeyed and leaned against the
breakwater she was sitting on.

'You'll get your suit dirty,' she warned.

'I'd get even dirtier if I were to sit on there with
you.'

'Well, I don't have to stay immaculate. I'm not
about to have a honeymoon.' Gabrielle read the
apprehension in his face. 'You aren't going to have any
problems are you?'

'Goodness no. Everything functions reasonably
well considering what happened to it.'

'Good. I'd hate to see Penny disappointed.'

'Aren't you going to let me have my wedding
present now?' he asked.

'Oh? What did I promise you, apart from the
medical dictionary, then?'

'You promised to explain how you managed to save
me from the ultimate operation two months ago, before
some Watcher catches up with us.'

Gabrielle didn't reply.

He went on, 'I know you stopped those bullets.'

'You know about the Watchers?'

'Yes, of course. They are the ultimate law
enforcers. You'll soon be finding out about them for
yourself anyway.'

'Humour me. Go on.'

'They enforce the law by using symbols that can be
recognised by all sophisticated life forms. If the Law

isn't obeyed after one of these is issued...' He shrugged. 'They have the power of the Galaxy at their disposal. They probably are the Galaxy.'

Gabrielle raised an eyebrow.

Weatherby felt even more uncomfortable. 'They existed before the stars, and may have created them for all I know.'

'Now that is power.'

'They don't use it much because no one makes a habit of crossing them.' Then a chilling thought occurred to him. 'You haven't managed to contact a Watcher?'

'Not exactly.'

'Then how did you know about them?'

'Poor Toby might have developed the knowledge, but would have been too frightened to use it.' Gabrielle paused. 'Life is relative to its environment, space-time, or element. Spirits, as humans call them, exist in many forms. They pass from one incarnation to another, yet seldom leapt into existence from nothing. You were an exception. The first android to step onto the spiral of life.'

'How? I don't remember it suddenly arriving.'

'It is being investigated. You were not spared because you developed a human biology, but because you acquired a soul. No one knows where it came from, or if it will happen again.'

Despite himself, Weatherby began to shake. 'How do you know all this, Gabrielle?'

Gabrielle casually reached out to push her fingers through his tightly curled hair. 'Because, my dear stowaway, I am a Watcher.'

THE END